~~ saying
About Jack Patterson

"R.J. Patterson does a fantastic job at keeping you engaged and interested. I look forward to more from this talented author."
- *Aaron Patterson*
bestselling author of SWEET DREAMS

CROSS HAIRS

"Small town life in southern Idaho might seem quaint and idyllic to some. But when local newspaper reporter Cal Murphy begins to uncover a series of strange deaths that are linked to a sticky spider web of deception, the lid on the peaceful town is blown wide open. Told with all the energy and bravado of an old pro, first-timer R.J. Patterson hits one out of the park his first time at bat with *Cross Hairs*. It's that good."
- *Vincent Zandri*
bestselling author of THE REMAINS

"You can tell R.J. knows what it's like to live in the newspaper world, but with *Cross Hairs*, he's proven that he also can write one heck of a murder mystery."
- *Josh Katzowitz*
NFL writer for CBSSports.com
& *author of* Sid Gillman: Father of the Passing Game

"Patterson has a mean streak about a mile wide and puts his two main characters through quite a horrible ride, which makes for good reading."
- *Richard D.*, *reader*

CROSS THE LINE

"This book kept me on the edge of my seat the whole time. I didn't really want to put it down. R.J. Patterson has hooked me. I'll be back for more."

- Bob Behler
3-time Idaho broadcaster of the year
and play-by-play voice for Boise State football

"Like a John Grisham novel, from the very start I was pulled right into the story and couldn't put the book down. It was as if I personally knew and cared about what happened to each of the main characters. Every chapter ended with so much excitement and suspense I had to continue to read until I learned how it ended, even though it kept me up until 3:00 A.M.

- Ray F., reader

THE WARREN OMISSIONS

"What can be more fascinating than a super high concept novel that re-opens the conspiracy behind the JFK assassination while the threat of a global world war rests in the balance? With his new novel, *The Warren Omissions*, former journalist turned bestselling author R.J. Patterson proves he just might be the next worthy successor to Vince Flynn."

- Vincent Zandri
bestselling author of THE REMAINS

OTHER TITLES BY
R.J. PATTERSON

Cal Murphy Thrillers
Dead Shot
Dead Line
Better off Dead
Dead in the Water

James Flynn Thrillers
The Warren Omissions
Imminent Threat
The Cooper Affair
Seeds of War

THE WARREN OMISSIONS
© Copyright 2013 R.J. Patterson

This book is a work of fiction. Any references to historical events, real people, or real locales are used fictitiously. Other names, characters, places, and incidents are products of the author's imagination, and any resemblance to actual events or locales or persons, living or dead, is entirely coincidental.

First Edition 2013
Second Edition 2017

Cover Design by Dan Pitts

Published in the United States of America
Boise Idaho 83713

THE
WARREN
OMISSIONS

A James Flynn Thriller

R.J. PATTERSON

AUTHOR'S NOTE

Mixing fact and fiction can be an exciting venture—and a risky one, too. When I set out to tell this story, I didn't do so with the idea of creating a new theory on who was behind JFK's assassination. My extensive research on the subject leads me to believe—just like the findings from the House Select Committee on Assassions in 1978—that there was a conspiracy. After looking through the evidence, it's easy to understand why there are plenty of theories. However, instead of creating something new, I wanted to synthesize several theories in order to create a thrilling plot that could be considered plausible. I wouldn't dare pretend that the theory proffered in the pages ahead should be added to the lengthy list already out there, though that's entirely for you to decide as the reader. I hope you do nothing more than find the story entertaining—and thought provoking.

R.J. Patterson
Boise, Idaho
October 2013

To Pieter, your deserved to tell a real story like this

PROLOGUE

Luanda, Angola
April 1954

JOAQUIM BUSCAPE TAPPED HIS FOOT as he sat on the steps of his porch just beyond the reach of the rain. He swirled his glass, creating a circular current of rum. The darkness combined with the thrumming sound of raindrops on the roof should have soothed him. But it only created more angst for Joaquim. At least that's how he was known here. Just Joaquim. However, back in the heart of Angola's booming capital he was Father Buscape.

Joaquim peered down the road, awaiting the arrival of his visitor. He hated waiting, but he needed more time—more time to drink the liquid courage. Tonight, he needed it all.

In a way, this meeting represented a confession of sorts by Joaquim. He needed absolution from what he had done—and for what he was about to do. Despite being one of the most prominent non-political figures in Luanda, the house by the sea in Paisi do Bosos served as a necessary escape. The weight of presenting himself as a perfect model for his parishioners resulted in a painful existence, crushed beneath the watchful eyes of those seeking permission rather than transformation. They wanted to hear that their struggles were normal—and acceptable. Yet Father Buscape stood in stark contrast to their lifestyle. He appeared unblemished in every way, from his ruggedly handsome face atop his six-foot frame to the soles of his feet that trudged the streets serving the poor.

And for a time, Joaquim's outward actions mirrored the depth of his soul. He spent time with the orphans. He delivered food to the widows. He employed the jobless. Then one day, his perfection vanished.

Sixteen years ago, Father Buscape was visiting all the widows in the parish as usual. However, when he delivered some produce to Maria on his final stop, it was anything but usual. Maria was too young to be a widow. Her husband, Umberto, worked on a local fishing vessel. One day a vicious squall arose in the South Atlantic and decimated the boat. The storm swept Umberto off the deck and into the frothy waters. He never stood a chance. Maria was also far too beautiful to remain unmarried. Her long flowing brown hair framed her soft face. Her figure far too voluptuous to avoid leering glances. Her dark complexion accentuated her radiant blue eyes. And that's what made her stand out—those eyes. Father Buscape knew he shouldn't stare too deeply into her teary blue pools that day. Temptation never looked so beautiful; sin never seemed more right.

The silhouette of a man appeared in the distance, taking shape as it moved toward Joaquim. Absolution was nigh. To say that Joaquim looked forward to this day would be a mischaracterization. Most people look forward to something because it signals something new, something good. But for Joaquim, this meeting signaled something different. It would be good, but only on one hand—the evil hand that clutches dark secrets. His secret would all but disappear with the exit of the man steadily approaching him.

Joaquim stood up and turned toward the house.

"Are you ready?" he asked.

The boy standing in the doorway nodded.

Joaquim wasn't sure if Marcos really understood what was about to happen—but it needed to happen. This was a small sacrifice for what this meeting would mean about the future. Not just his future, but the world's future. Joaquim could maintain his position of influence and expand it to include something he truly believed in, something he viewed as equal to his faith in God: communism.

Over the last 15 years, war had ravaged every corner of the world. The unquenchable thirst for power did more to destroy the world's good trust in mankind than any atomic bomb ever did. Now, there was a different war, a war over the ideology that would rule in the near future. Democracies and republics seemed poised to prevail, but Joaquim recognized that people left unto themselves would eventually destroy each other. Mankind needed a firm hand to rule them, but a compassionate, caring hand as well. People needed strict guidelines. They also needed provision. A government that could provide both elements just might lead to the world Joaquim hoped to see, the kind of world he spoke passionately about in his homilies: a global cooperative community. Or as it was more commonly known—communism.

When a man who shared Joaquim's deepest convictions contacted him, Joaquim couldn't refuse the meeting. Nor could he resist joining forces. The man's passion burned with a white-hot glow. He would do anything for the greater cause of establishing communism in the world. And he wanted to know if Joaquim would do the same. If Joaquim agreed to certain conditions, the man would finance the establishment of the communist party in Angola. Joaquim would share the leadership with his activist brother, Mário—and Joaquim could save his parishioners' souls ... and their futures.

Joaquim watched as the man sloshed through the many shallow holes pooling with muddy water. He walked deliberately up the steps and nodded at his host. Though the darkness prevented Joaquim from fully inspecting his visitor, he could see that the man's face had begun to weather. He displayed signs of a warrior who engaged in battle, but not fierce battles. Those would lie ahead. That's why he needed help. That's why he needed Joaquim's son.

The man turned toward the boy.

"Is this him?" the man asked. His thick accent revealed his Russian roots.

"Yes. He's all yours," Joaquim responded.

The man nodded at Marcos and reached out his hand to reassure. He needed the boy's trust or it would be for naught.

Marcos moved toward the man before stopping. He turned and hugged his father, a short embrace that ended with one firm pat on the back. No lingering. It was a clear parting of ways.

"You know I love you," Joaquim added.

Marcos nodded yet said nothing.

"I will see that he gets everything he needs," the man said. "And don't worry—I will take care of your son."

The man turned and walked down the steps with Marcos in tow.

Joaquim watched as they walked away into the darkness, his vision blurred by the steady rain. As their figures quickly vanished, Joaquim couldn't decipher the rain from his tears. He wondered what kind of monster he had become. He questioned the cost of his cause. But tomorrow would be different. Tomorrow, Joaquim would be Father Buscape forevermore.

But tomorrow was still a day away. His secret was not yet safe. And it wouldn't be until he finished burying Maria's body in a place it would never be found.

CHAPTER 1

Present Day

JAMES FLYNN WRESTLED with his computer bag as he exited the terminal. A long walk awaited him before he arrived at his transportation. Flynn stared at the awkward innards of Washington National Airport, partially out of intrigue over the cavernous structure, partially out of his insatiable desire to know where every surveillance camera pointed. He believed the architecture, conceived and constructed in a bygone era, served as a microcosm of this city built on ambition. People in D.C. lived to leave a mark on the world, from the most crooked of politicians to the taxi cab driver on a 4 a.m. shift. Some architect likely fancied that his architecture would be adored by millions who flew into the nation's capital via Washington National. However, Flynn thought every era demanded a closer look. He viewed nostalgia as a complicit accomplice in covering up our nation's sins, sins he was determined to expose.

Nearing the exit to the metro, Flynn felt someone tap him on the shoulder. He spun around to see one of his adoring fans. He knew it before the man even uttered a word. The scraggily brown beard, thinning mop of hair, and baggy jeans held all the telltale signs. But it was the ragged red t-shirt with the schematics of the Millennium Falcon from Star Wars that instantly alerted Flynn to the direction of this conversation.

"Dr. Flynn? I'm Harold Baylor," the man said, offering his hand.

Flynn shook the man's hand and forced a smile. "Nice to meet you, Harold."

"I'm one of your biggest fans," Harold said. "Your story about how Reagan spied on Mondale during the election was fascinating."

"Thanks, Harold."

Then Harold leaned in close to Flynn and put his hand up near his mouth in preparation to share a secret moment. "Now if you can just figure out who killed JFK?"

Flynn withdrew from Harold and smiled. Flynn then glanced around and then leaned in to share a secret moment of his own with Harold. "Oh, I'm sure if I try to solve that one, my life will meet an untimely demise."

Harold's eyes transformed from squinty and beady to large saucers. He wiped clean any hint of a smile.

"Well, be careful, Dr. Flynn. Nice meeting you." Harold hiked up sagging jeans with one hand and turned toward the airport entrance.

Flynn gritted his teeth, politely smiled and waved while Harold trudged away. Though Flynn preferred more anonymity, his regular appearances on cable news talk shows ended those wishes.

Two years ago, Flynn achieved celebrity status when he uncovered evidence that Ronald Reagan followed in the footsteps of Richard Nixon by utilizing government resources to spy on his presidential opponent. Reagan supporters rushed to their hero's defense, seeking to destroy Flynn's credibility. They deemed the evidence as fake. They questioned Flynn's motives. They dug up dirt on his personal life. Typical Washington tactics. None of it bothered Flynn. He endured much worse from much more powerful people.

The fact that Flynn was now writing for *The International* magazine instead of still serving as an intelligence operative for the CIA proved the worst had already been done to him. Serving in the Middle East beginning in 2002, Flynn's contribution to the war on terror was discreet. He went under the cover of an English teacher, which is what he did in various countries. But at night, he analyzed intel, translating recorded conversations within terror cells. It made Flynn feel like he was leaving a mark on the world. It might not be as visible as an architect's airport, but it was saving lives by helping the military eliminate enemy combatants.

Then his sense of importance crumbled when he stumbled across a recording that revealed a rouge Marine strapped a bomb to a 10-year-old Iraqi boy just to prove that their presence in one sector of Iraq was necessary. Flynn still winced when forced to recall the moment he learned of this atrocity committed by a fellow countryman. He struggled with what to do with this information, weighing the cost of his decision to report it. When he finally concluded that he couldn't be complicit in a cover-up, he reported the incident. Senior officials assured him it would be dealt with internally. But after two months, nothing happened. The soldier continued to serve on his post without any consequence.

Enraged that nothing was done, Flynn spoke with his superiors again. They justified their inaction by explaining that the Abu Graib prison incident was sufficient embarrassment for the American military and that exposing this might result in rioting by Muslim extremists. Flynn threatened to go over their heads—then he was dismissed.

Flynn sought out the help of a journalist friend who wrote a story about the incident, based on Flynn's account, for *The Washington Times*. But everything Flynn said was dismissed, as government officials painted a nasty picture of Flynn: disgruntled after being passed over for promotion; poor performance reviews; faulty intel reports that resulted in the loss of innocent civilian lives. None of it was true, but they cooked up enough official documents to force *The Washington Times* to issue a retraction.

With nearly every bridge burned, Flynn turned his intelligence skills to the only profession he could truly be appreciated—and universally reviled: journalism. More specifically, investigative journalism. After Flynn discovered the files that proved "Reagan-gate," his popularity soared. He proffered a few more government conspiracies and achieved rock star status among those who were leery of the government. Even www.TinFoilHatConspiracy.com recently named Flynn their conspiracy theorist of the year. Now whenever there was a conspiracy theory hatched, cable news talk shows clamored to be the first to get Flynn on their sets. It wasn't a big mark, but it was something. His story on Reagan was toothless in the fact that it was learned long after Reagan's death. Had Flynn been a reporter and discovered this while Reagan was still in the White House, he would've been immortalized. Instead, he was still in search of his Woodward and Bernstein moment. And that was exactly why Flynn found himself standing in D.C. today, braving the chilling October winds on the Metro platform.

Three days ago, Flynn received a call from a woman named Emma Taylor. She told him it was urgent and needed to meet with him pertaining a document her grandfather willed to her. Flynn had grown accustomed to such calls. The conspiracy theorists often called him about leads and requested that he pay them a visit. But those visits were on his dime, unless he could convince *The International* that there really was a story to be written. Most of the time, Flynn politely declined the invitation. After crisscrossing the country a few times chasing bogus leads from people with fanciful imaginations, he wised up as he watched his bank account dwindle. Yet Flynn didn't dismiss them all. He developed a handful of subjects and names that required more questions before he would agree to a visit. This latest call happened to fulfill his criteria.

Squeezing through the Monday rush hour traffic, Flynn boarded the Branch Avenue rail line and sat in a seat at the back of the car. He felt anxious, something foreign to him since he left the agency. Anxious about what this document might mean; anxious that perhaps someone was following him. Based on his conversation with Mrs. Taylor, this document more than met his requirement for a personal visit. If this wasn't *the* document, with one or two more it certainly could comprise that elusive smoking gun, the holy grail for every investigative journalist: Who was behind the JFK assassination plot?

Flynn got off at Navy Yard metro station and walked toward the address given to him by Mrs. Taylor. Flynn loved the Capitol Hill neighborhood since it served as a splendid smorgasbord of architecture. Several years ago, the city's revitalization projection on 8th Street resulted in crafty restorations of older buildings and the introduction of more modern designs. Trendy restaurants and savvy boutique stores gulped up the available commercial sites and the bustle returned. That and well-lit streets attracted younger professionals and returned the area to its former glory. Based on what Flynn knew about the area, he expected to find a young woman in her mid- to late 20s. She likely either worked as a professional in D.C. or was attending law school like everyone else in this town.

A stained oak door held the numbers for the address given to Flynn. He walked up the steps and grabbed the knocker held in the mouth of a cast iron lion.

Flynn heard the clicking of heels on a hardwood floor before the drawn out creak of the solid door opening. Instantly, he surmised she was a young business professional. She wore her smooth dark hair up in a bun. Her plain gray skirt and non-descript white blouse were only accented by gray-patterned hose and burgundy heels. She appeared as if she had just arrived home from work.

"Hi, Ms. Taylor. I'm James Flynn from *The International.*"

"Please, won't you come in?" she asked, gesturing inside.

Flynn stepped through the doorway and held his coat in his hand. She offered to take it for him, suggesting this conversation was going to last a while. He wanted to make her comfortable with him and figured some small talk might be good

In a short amount of time, Flynn's pointed line of questioning revealed that Ms. Taylor worked as a curator at the Smithsonian's National Science Museum, and had so for the past four years. She had recently graduated from George Washington University and decided to stay in America's power city. Flynn guessed she was about twenty-eight years old, based on her graduation date, her time spent at the museum and her stint in Jordan with the Peace Corps.

As captivating as her life might be, Flynn was really only interested in seeing if this document was worth the money he plunked down for the ticket to D.C.

"So, tell me about this document, Ms. Taylor," Flynn began.

"Please, call me Emma," she said.

"Okay, Emma. What's the story? Why call me?"

Emma picked up a manilla folder and her hands began to tremble.

"I called you because I didn't know who else to call. After living in D.C. for about eight years now, I've learned to trust no one in this town."

"I understand. I'm sure your grandfather felt the same way," Flynn added, trying to sound reassuring.

"I also followed the story about you in the news several years ago—and I knew you could handle this information better than anyone else."

Flynn studied Emma's eyes as they scanned the room nervously. Before the trip, Flynn had a good feeling about this evidence. Now, his hopes were sky high that this secret document that Emma held in her hand truly was something big and well worth the trip.

"So, what is this?" Flynn asked, gesturing toward the folder.

"This is something my grandfather left my father, but my father never opened it. In fact, this folder had been sitting in a safety deposit box for more than 35 years until I retrieved it recently. My father said that any secrets his dad had were the kind that get you killed—but I think that's ridiculous. His dad worked for the CIA, so I guess it's easy to understand why he was so easily spooked."

"Does anyone know about these files?"

"Nobody but me and you. At least, I haven't told anyone else about them."

Flynn was getting tired of waiting.

"So, let's take a peek. What are we looking at here?"

Emma flipped open the folder, exposing a handful of CIA documents. The papers were dated 1963 and 1964, and the frayed edges and smeared ink confirmed that these documents were produced in the bygone era of carbon copies—stray marks on the page, arcane correction methods.

Flynn couldn't read fast enough, but he wanted an immediate summary. It didn't take long for Emma to blurt it out.

"These are papers from the CIA's investigation in the JFK assassination."

Flynn's heart sunk. He had spent weeks at the archives and had combed through thousands of documents in the JFK assassination collection—FBI files, CIA documents, reports from the House Select Committee on Assassinations. Most of the pieces seemed to be there, but there were always a few key pieces missing. Everyone who proposed they knew who the mastermind conspirator was behind JFK's death always failed to definitively prove their theory. Some powerful person in the government was like the kid who hides two or three pieces of a puzzle so he can put the last pieces on the board—except these people never had any intention of letting anyone complete the puzzle. He expected this to lead nowhere.

Flynn said nothing as he sifted through the files, trying to determine if this was just another expensive trip he wouldn't be able to justify to his editor.

"There's this one strange graph in the back... I have no idea what it means," she said, grabbing the last few sheets at the bottom of the pile of papers.

She shoved them in front of Flynn. He instantly recognized the form. It was a polygraph test.

At the top of the file was a handwritten name: "Gilberto Alvarado Ugarte."

Flynn knew all about Ugarte and his allegations in Mexico City in the days following the assassination of JFK. He began explaining to Emma how Ugarte claimed to have seen a man matching the description of Lee Harvey Oswald in Mexico City with a man in possession of a Canadian passport, as well as a "red-haired negro" two months prior to the assassination. It was a settled fact that Lee Harvey Oswald was in Mexico City on September 28, but Ugarte's date was off by 10 days. The CIA quickly dismissed Ugarte's testimony when he recanted, claiming that as an operative of the Nicaraguan military trying to infiltrate Mexico, he made up the claims to get in the good graces of the United States. He then recanted his initial recant, saying the Mexican government pressured him to recant his story. It all seemed like a rabbit trail until Mexican poet Elena Garro corroborated Ugarte's story. She claimed to have seen Lee Harvey Oswald with the same company on the correct date. Garro was dismissed as a nut case and her eyewitness account was also dismissed in the initial report by the Warren Commission.

Flynn concluded his explanation by glancing at the polygraph test in front of him. He put his hand to his mouth, expressing utter awe at the information divulged on the polygraph test. The polygraph affirmed that he was telling the truth on every question. But in the CIA's official report, Ugarte was shown to have been lying on four questions:

* Did you see a large sum of money on September 18?
* Did you see this money given to a person you described as Oswald?
* In the Cuban Consulate, did you hear someone say, "$6,500"?
* Did you hear someone say, "I can kill him"?

Flynn saw the handwritten note from Emma's grandfather, explaining how the question "Did you see a large sum of money on September 18?" was interpreted incorrectly. The question was actually asked about September 28. And Ugarte passed. Another note explained that he passed the other questions, too.

Emma finally asked the only question that mattered in this titillating piece of evidence: "What does all this mean?"

"In and of itself, nothing," Flynn replied. "The House Select Committee on Assassinations conceded that JFK's death was likely a conspiracy and that Lee Harvey Oswald was acting on the orders of others. But since Ugarte's testimony is true, the most important aspect of this story that needs to be investigated is determining who were the men with Lee Harvey Oswald that night. That might actually reveal who was behind JFK's assassination."

Emma stared blankly at Flynn before finally breaking the heavy silence.

"Wow," she said. "This is obviously something big."

"Yes, this is the Holy Grail of all modern-day conspiracies. And this just might be the clue to help point us in the right direction."

Flynn requested to take pictures of the entire contents of the folder, a request that Emma granted.

When he finished, Flynn advised Emma to return the files to the safety deposit box and to not speak of them to anyone. She nodded, as if she agreed. Flynn thanked Emma and promised her that he would include her in his acknowledgments should he ever write a book about this one day. He bid her a good evening and walked back to the Metro, lost in thought over the evidence he had just discovered.

***

FLYNN'S RETURN FLIGHT to New York was scheduled for 2 p.m. on Tuesday, affording him the opportunity to sleep in. But that ended abruptly at 9:00 a.m. when his cell phone began buzzing.

"Hello?" Flynn said groggily.

"Is this James Flynn?" a voice asked.

"Yes. Who is this?"

"I'm Greg Harper of the D.C. police department. We need you to come in for questioning."

"Come in for questioning? What on earth for?"

"Do you know a Ms. Emma Taylor?"

"Sure. I met with her last night about a story I'm working on. Is everything OK?"

"I'm afraid it's not, Mr. Flynn. She was murdered this morning as she was walking to her car."

"What?!"

"You heard me. And we need to speak with you since we suspect you were the last person who saw her alive."

"Why in the world would you say that?"

"Her Twitter feed. Last night she posted, 'Who killed JFK? My grandpa knew and a new friend is going to solve the case.' She also included your Twitter handle, @TheJamesFlynn.

"I told her not to tell anyone about our meeting," Flynn said, still stunned by the news.

"Maybe you should have told her not to tell *everyone*," Harper quipped.

Flynn promised Harper he would speak with him and hung up. Despite feeling sorrow over Emma Taylor's early demise, Flynn leaked a wry smile. He thumbed through the pictures he had taken the night before on his iPhone. He was going to find out who really killed JFK.

CHAPTER 2

GERALD SANDFORD STARED at his itinerary for the day. In his late 50s, he certainly looked the part of a statesman. Handsome, rugged good looks. Big green eyes and a distinct chin. A full head of hair that had started to gray, projecting him as a wise man. And at a shade just below six-feet, two inches, he exuded power when he walked in a room. But he wasn't feeling so powerful as he perused his itinerary. Just below the tagline "The Office of the Vice President of the United States of America" was the date: October 2. Just another day for most people, but not for Sandford. Sixteen years ago on October 2, his daughter, Sydney, was killed.

Sandford paused and reflected on his daughter's life. Sydney had just graduated from college and wanted to see the world, specifically Russia. Volunteering with the Peace Corps, she was one of the first workers to get into the country once it opened its doors to the global organization after the fall of the Iron Curtain. The letters Sydney sent home—and smiling pictures with friends, both fellow co-workers and new acquaintances, dancing, singing or partying together—suggested that Sydney was living her dream of worldwide peace.

But then the unthinkable happened. Chechnyan rebels stormed the school where Sydney was teaching, killing scores of students and teachers. Rebels forced students and teachers into an assembly hall before locking the doors and setting off enough explosives to bring down an entire sports stadium, according to Russian officials. Most of the remains couldn't be identified.

Sandford slammed his fist onto his desk and screamed out a slew of expletives. He and his wife tried to move on but it was difficult. Every October 2nd, he struggled with the reality that he would never see his daughter smile again, never hug her, never walk her down the aisle or watch her become a mother. All of these simple dreams were stolen from him. And they were stolen because of some ridiculous conflict, agitated by a group with blatant disregard for human life.

Sandford's secretary, Abbey Pearson, knocked on the door and entered once Sandford gave her permission.

"Is everything all right, Mr. Sandford?" Abbey asked.

"Oh, yes, I'm fine," he answered, sounding as if he didn't even believe himself. "What do you need?"

"Oh, nothing important," Abbey said. "I just had a few personal letters for you."

She slid a handful of envelopes on his desk and exited the room.

Sandford welcomed the distraction. Anything to take his mind off what today meant. Anything to take his mind off politics.

When Sandford came to Washington more than twenty years ago, he thought he could make a difference, influence change, return Capitol Hill to a place of significance by rediscovering the heart of what the forefathers wanted for the American people. It didn't take long for him to feel out of place. Washington had become a cesspool, a city where bare-knuckled politics supplanted statesmanship. Sandford hated it, all of it. The phony smiles, the political posturing, the "principled" decisions.

After Sydney died, Sandford mulled returning to normal life. There was almost no reason to stay and fight an unwinnable war. Yet there was one big reason: justice for Sydney. The Russian government never caught the rebels who killed his daughter. He blamed them as much as he blamed the rebels. Justice would never be served, not like it needed to be. Those men needed to pay for what they did to Sydney, for what they stole from him. And he was going to make sure somebody did one day.

That was all the motivation Sandford needed to stay in Washington. It drove his every decision, his every plan. Now it had taken him to the office of the Vice President. And if everything stayed on course, he would run as his party's presidential nomination in three years. That was still a big *if*, especially considering how he was on shaky terms with the President. Their public disagreements over policies often made front-page news, but Sandford knew, like most things in Washington, it would blow over eventually.

He glanced at his itinerary again. October 2 glared back at him. He shoved the paper aside and shuffled through the envelopes Abbey had placed on his desk. One envelope caught Sandford's eyes. His name was hand-written on the outside. No return address, no markings. Simply his name. Another staffer must have shoved this into his box in the mailroom.

He scrounged around in his drawer for his letter opener and ripped the envelope open. Sandford unfolded the piece of paper and read the note. Its message chilled him. It also excited him. Six words that meant his life could dramatically change. It read:

Are you ready to become President?

Sandford wanted to find out if Abbey knew who sent this note. Then he decided against it. If he had learned anything in Washington it was that culpable deniability was one of your greatest assets. He pulled a lighter out of his desk drawer and held the note in his hand before setting it on fire. The fire crept up the page, turning it into ash as it climbed near Sandford's thumb and forefinger that pinched the corner. As the flame drew closer, he blew it out and watched the ashes sprinkle into his trash can. He knew nothing—yet he was desperate to know more.

CHAPTER 3

FLYNN LOATHED TALKING TO COPS. After working for the world's best spy agency, all other law enforcement personnel made Flynn gape at their incompetency. They always went after obvious connections, ones that took no training on how to uncover who was behind a crime. And when it came to local law enforcement, Flynn surmised maybe that was a good thing. Most criminals are stupid and incompetent, leaving a trail of clues more obvious than Hansel and Gretel's breadcrumbs. He never understood how police procedurals became so popular on American television. It was the same thing over and over and over again. Local detectives might as well be working in a factory making auto parts all day. When Flynn entered the Washington, D.C. precinct handling Emma Taylor's murder investigation, he didn't have high expectations that anyone would have any idea what was really going on.

Flynn alerted a woman officer behind the front desk that he was summoned by Detective Alex Livingston to talk about a murder investigation. She called Livingston, and moments later he emerged. Unlike the uniformed officers, Livingston sported khaki slacks and a light blue button-down shirt. His brown hair slightly unkempt, Livingston offered Flynn his left hand to shake, refusing to transfer his coffee mug from his right hand. Flynn obliged with an awkward shake before following Livingston back to an office.

The name on the outside read, "Detective Ken Mooney." Flynn inquired why they were going to another detective's office. Livingston said that he needed a more private space to talk and his office was located in a more public spot. Flynn appreciated the gesture.

As soon as Flynn sat down, Livingston started with the questions.

"So, what were you doing at Ms. Taylor's house last night?" Livingston asked.

"Before we begin, I must ask if all of this is going to go into your official report because if it is, I can't tell you everything," Flynn responded.

"I'll put whatever I want in this report—and you better answer my questions straight. Just remember that you were the last person she was seen with last night."

"With all due respect, Detective Livingston, your empty threats are the last thing I'm worried about. If you put some of the things I tell you in your report, I'll be dead in a week. So, you can either leave some details out and we can continue. Or this conversation is over."

Flynn knew he was pushing the detective's buttons. But he'd do anything to shorten this torture.

"Fine, then," Livingston conceded. "What were you doing at Ms. Taylor's house last night?"

"She contacted me about some documents she wanted to give me."

"Documents pertaining to JFK's death, I presume?"

"You can presume all you want, but I'm not going on the record with that."

Livingston jotted down a few notes and continued.

"What was the nature of your relationship with Ms. Taylor?"

Flynn furrowed his brow and stared at Livingston. *Man, does this guy watch too many cop shows.*

"I told you that she contacted me because she wanted to give me something."

"Yes, but she stated on Twitter that you were friends."

Flynn shifted in his seat and sighed.

"Look, she was excited to meet me. I do have fans, you know. But I had never met her before."

"Yet you met at her private residence?"

"Yes, she had some documents that she didn't want anyone to see, not in public anyway. So she suggested that we meet at her place."

"What time did you leave Ms. Taylor's place?"

"I wasn't there more than thirty minutes. Maybe seven-thirty. I don't know for sure."

"Can you tell me for certain?"

"How did you even know I was there?"

"Other than your admission now? Surveillance cameras in the neighborhood captured you going into her house."

"So, wouldn't the surveillance cameras have the time I came out of her home?"

Livingston refused to look up, scribbling something in the corner of his pad. Flynn rolled his eyes in disgust and continued. "What kind of questions are these anyway? You already have all the answers to everything you're asking me."

"Just answer the question, Mr. Flynn."

"I already did."

"What did you do after you left?"

"I went straight back to my hotel and went over my notes from our conversation. Then I went downstairs and had a drink in the bar before retiring to my room for the evening."

"What time were you in the bar?"

"About ten o'clock."

"Can anyone verify you were there?"

"Yes, plenty of people." Flynn grew more agitated with each amateurish question. "Are we done here? I think it's pretty obvious I didn't kill her and I know nothing else."

"Fine. We're done. But I don't want you leaving town for a week. I may need to bring you back in for more questioning."

Flynn huffed as he grabbed his briefcase and walked out of the office. He didn't like the order to stay around in Washington, but he didn't put up much of a fuss. It would be a good excuse to stay and do more research without his editor climbing all over him. Flynn glanced around the office to see if anyone was watching him. Nobody looked suspicious, but that didn't mean he wasn't being watched. He exited the building, looking over his shoulder one last time.

***

INSIDE THE PRECINCT, Livingston waited until Flynn left the building. He stared out the window until he observed Flynn crossing the street below. He fished out his cell phone from his pants pocket and placed a call.

"So, what did you find out?" the voice on the other end asked.

"I don't think he knows anything, but you can never be too sure. I told him not to leave town for a week, so we should be able to figure out what he knows by then."

"Good. Keep an eye on him. We can't have him revealing more secrets. And if he does, I have a man who can take care of him."

CHAPTER 4

IVAN STOOD ON THE Washington street corner surveying his next victim. He wasn't exactly proud of what he did. No one ever really grows up with aspirations of becoming an assassin. But such labels disgusted Ivan. He prided himself on being part of a cause, something bigger than himself. And the cause needed him. More precisely, they needed his dedication.

Ivan could count on two hands the number of people he killed while serving the cause. They were brutal murders too. He once killed a man by dragging him behind a truck on a dirt road for three miles, traveling 60 miles an hour. He cut the man loose and tossed his body into the woods for the animals to devour. Another one of his signature kills came when he choked a man to death by cutting off the man's fingers and ramming them down his throat until he couldn't breathe. But it wasn't how he killed his victims that earned him the nickname, Ivan the Terrible—a nickname he hated. No, it was how he tortured them. Sometimes he killed them. Sometimes they would kill themselves—anything to avoid a second of torture at his hands. But when you're six-foot-four with a weightlifter physique, you have a presence that frightens most people with your mere appearance.

As he watched the man across the street, he wondered if it would ever come to that point. He preferred to persuade and cajole people to do what he wanted them to do. His moral appeals often found acceptance in a society full of people who wanted to do right. However, what seemed right to him didn't always seem right to others. That resistant attitude required a different type of persuasion, the kind of persuasion that earned him his nickname and made others fear him. He hoped his next victim would succumb to simple persuasion.

He popped his collar up on his blue athletic warm-up jacket and followed his assignment. Being careful to stay far enough back to avoid being seen was an art he perfected. A Nationals baseball cap and large sunglasses helped Ivan blend into the Washington streets. Who wasn't wearing a Nationals cap these days? He'd even seen a few senators sport them before yanking them off at the last minute and dashing into the Capitol. This is what he did—observe. He needed to gain every possible access point to his victims without being identified. He needed to be a ghost.

As he meandered behind his target, he realized the guy was a pro. Very aware of his surroundings, the man kept looking over his shoulder in Ivan's direction. Ivan grew uneasy with the constant checking and jumped in a cab. It was one thing to identify someone following you on foot. But it took a specially trained person to realize someone in a car was following you. Ivan doubted the man was *that* special.

Ivan instructed the cab driver to follow the man on foot but not get too close. The driver let out an exasperated sigh but complied, staying far enough away that the man on foot never seemed to identify them as slowly following him along the streets of Washington. After ten minutes, Ivan realized his victim was headed into a hotel. He ordered the cab driver to stop so he could chase the man down. Throwing a $20 bill at the driver, Ivan dashed across the street in pursuit of the man.

Without a second to spare, Ivan managed to catch the man just before he stepped onto an elevator in The Liaison hotel lobby. He tapped him on the shoulder.

"Excuse me, Mr. Flynn," Ivan said. "May I have a moment of your time?"

***

FLYNN SPUN AROUND to see the same man he spotted the moment he came out of the police precinct nearly twenty minutes earlier. He certainly wasn't a fan since the man was well skilled in tailing someone. Flynn suspected he might be after him, but couldn't conceive why.

Maybe he was CIA or FBI. Flynn couldn't be sure. The only certainty was that the man standing in front of him now had tailed him to this point and had impeded Flynn from getting on an elevator.

"What can I do for you?" Flynn asked, doing his best to act as if the man's interruption was a completely delightful surprise.

"Well, I'm a big fan of your books, Mr. Flynn, and I wanted to give you something that you might find interesting."

Flynn did his best to act as if this was all the conversation was about. "Oh? What is it?" he asked.

The man held a folder leaned in close, speaking slightly above a whisper.

"This is a group of documents that shows how the CIA created the Bay of Pigs crisis. It wasn't an accident. It was a well thought out and planned operation. And the American people have never known the truth about what happened during that time. I thought you might be the one to tell them."

Flynn tried not to act too excited. First the JFK assassination, now the Bay of Pigs? If this was real, he'd have his next two book deals set. Somehow Flynn wondered if the man wasn't trying to throw him off. Could the man's information be trusted, especially since he spoke with a thick accent—an accent he struggled to place?

The man moved to hand the folder to Flynn before it slipped out of his hand and spilled onto the floor. He apologized to Flynn as the two men knelt down and scooped up the pages.

"Thank you for this. I appreciate it," Flynn said as he stood up. "What's your name again? I didn't catch it."

"It's not important," the man said. "In fact, it's best that you not know me. Good bye."

He patted Flynn on the shoulder before turning and walking away, leaving the folder in Flynn's hands.

***

IVAN HEARD THE ELEVATOR BELL ring again, signaling its arrival. He didn't turn around to look back at Flynn. He only smiled, reveling in his two-fold victory.

His cause didn't like the idea of anyone getting close to figuring out who they were. They also preferred to use every other means necessary to persuade people rather than murder. Murder was messy and created more problems. More trails. More nosy people sniffing around in places they shouldn't be. The CIA knew about them and that was more than enough.

Unfortunately, Emma Taylor required the messy kind of removal. Conspiracy theorists would use her untimely demise as a way of pointing out that her death had something to do with JFK's assassination plot, based on her final tweet. But nobody ever believed those people anyway. They thought everything that happened was somehow related to an overarching government conspiracy to keep the public in the dark. Most of the time they were right. Yet Emma Taylor needed to be dealt with—and she was private enough of a person that her murder looked like a mugging gone wrong. At least, that's how Ivan made it look.

But he couldn't stop smiling as he walked away from his "chance" meeting with James Flynn. Not only did he deliver him papers that were sure to make him ditch his digging into the JFK assassination plot, but he also managed to swipe his phone and plant a bug on it. It was simple really. A surprise touch on the shoulder always gave him access to snatch whatever he was after. Then an accidental drop of the papers gave him all the time he needed to switch out Flynn's phone cover with one embedded with a bug. All without Flynn knowing it. Even a trained CIA operative like Flynn couldn't detect his sleight of hand. The tricks he learned growing up on the streets of Moscow served him well now.

If Flynn now decided to restart his investigation into who was behind the JFK assassination, Ivan would know about it immediately. Not that it would matter soon.

CHAPTER 5

FLYNN WAITED UNTIL HE WAS in his room with the door shut before he began thumbing through the papers handed to him by the mystery man. For most people, this would be a rare occurrence, perhaps a once-in-a-lifetime event. But this happened to Flynn all the time. His public image made him a dumping ground for every tin foil hat-wearing nut job. Theories about Area 51 scratched out on a bar napkin were handed to him in an airport. Strangers accosted him with doctorate-level dissertations about how NASA faked the moon landing. Others emailed grainy pictures showing proof of life of everything—from Jimmy Hoffa to Sasquatch. It was enough to make most people crazy. But not Flynn. He enjoyed the ideas, knowing shards of truth were lodged in the bevy of theories. Just pull each string until someone sings. It just took patience and a relentless commitment to uncovering believable evidence to posit on the public.

The documents on the Bay of Pigs invasion were interesting, but nothing to distract him from his main pursuit. Perhaps it was a smoke screen, designed to throw him off the trail. If whoever this man was thought a conspiracy about the Bay of Pigs was going to derail his pursuit of JFK's assassination, he had severely underestimated Flynn's resolve. However, Flynn wouldn't waste the information. He called his editor, Theresa Halston, and told her that he learned some interesting things about the Bay of Pigs invasion that might make for a nice cover story. He told her that he had to stay in Washington per the orders of local law enforcement and could use the time to dig into the story a little more. Flynn received an earful from a disgusted editor who vowed to call the detective and raise "holy hell" if he wasn't released to leave immediately. He passed along the number on Detective Livingston's card so she could follow up on her promise. Flynn smiled as he said good-bye before hanging up. If there's one thing he appreciated about Theresa, it was her loyalty to her reporters.

Spending years serving as a spy, Flynn never could shake those habits ingrained in him by the agency. Protocol for speaking on the phone when you suspected your room might be bugged was to go into a bathroom and turn the water on. If there was an overhead fan, all the better. Anything to muffle your voice. But Flynn added his own precautions, starting with the purchase of a burner phone. He knew either a spy or a criminal came up with this brilliant idea. Even the NSA couldn't track burner phones purchased in cash. Flynn purchased a new one each month, writing it off on his expense report. He reasoned with Theresa that it was actually a cost-saving method since he never saddled the magazine with his personal phone bill. With Theresa unconvinced, Flynn went on to say that it prevented the government from obtaining his phone records and putting his sources at risk. Apparently, that was enough to win her approval and add it to Flynn's monthly expense account. Flynn knew just how much snooping the government did—and he feared what might happen to his sources if he ever broke a story that was big enough to truly upset higher-ups in the federal government.

Once Flynn prepared the bathroom, he pulled out his burner phone, hoping that Natalie Hart wouldn't be on her lunch break yet. Several years before, Flynn met Natalie at the National Archives while working on a research piece about Pearl Harbor. She seemed eager to help him on his story, even bending the rules and helping him sneak a few papers out one night. She trusted him to return them, which he did. That week kindled a new friendship, one Flynn hoped might evolve into something more some day.

As good as he was at reading people when it came to telling the truth, Flynn failed miserably when trying to determine if a woman liked him romantically or not. Natalie often twirled her long brunette locks with her fingers while talking with him. *Was that a sign that she likes me or a nervous twitch?* Flynn never could be sure. The only thing he was sure of was that he liked her. He enjoyed her company at dinner, an event that Flynn made sure happened every time he was in town if staying for more than a couple of days. Yet he feared if he pressed the issue with her that she might decline any forward advances and ruin their current platonic relationship. *I can stare a combatant in the face pointing a gun at me without blinking but I can't get up the courage to give Natalie a goodnight kiss.* Flynn couldn't be more embarrassed over that fact. But it never stopped him from asking her out to dinner when he was in town.

He dialed her number and listened to the rings. On the third ring, she picked up. She sounded glad to hear from him and hinted that she had no plans for dinner that evening. After quickly planning to meet up for dinner, Flynn told her the second reason for his call.

"I also was wondering if you could authenticate a document for me," Flynn said.

"Oh, what kind of document?"

"An FBI document from a polygraph test."

"Still trying to solve who was behind JFK's assassination, are we?"

"How did you know?"

Natalie chuckled. "When it comes to asking me for favors, that's the only subject that ever pops up with you. Are you ever going to give this up?"

Flynn sighed. "You know my obsession all too well. And since it's an obsession, I probably never will—at least until I find out who was behind it all."

"I'll tell you what," Natalie said. "I've got some free time this afternoon and I'll be happy to take a look at it for you. Just bring it on down."

"Is a copy fine?"

"If all you've got is a copy, why don't you just email it to me?"

"Are you crazy? My email connected to your government account with a top secret document leading to who was behind the JFK assassination? I don't want you to be found floating in the Potomac River next week."

Natalie laughed. "How chivalrous of you. OK, fine. Bring it down on your phone or computer or whatever. We'll look at it without linking my account to yours so I don't end up as fish food."

Flynn was relieved. He knew more than a half dozen reporters who died of strange circumstances when they began digging into JFK's assassination. He wasn't about to put Natalie—or himself—at risk. Not when something potentially as big as this found its way into his hands.

***

STAYING DOWNTOWN WASHIINGTON at The Liaison, Flynn made the short one-mile walk to the National Archives. He didn't sit down to eat lunch, instead grabbing a hot dog from a street vendor as he walked. Natalie consumed his thoughts, so much so that he passed on the onions, which was his favorite garnishment. He couldn't wait to see her again, though he knew his stomach would knot up. He often wondered how anyone could have such a physiological effect on him. Pushing those thoughts aside, Flynn went over a few one-liners he heard in the movies that earned a laugh from the ladies in the audience. He picked one out that he liked before beginning to wonder if they were laughing because it was absurd or because they thought it was charming. Undecided, Flynn decided to ditch the charm and compliment her on her clothes or hair before jumping into business.

Upon reaching the downtown branch of the National Archives, Flynn waited five minutes for the hourly shuttle that transported researchers to the archives branch in Annapolis. While the downtown building was iconic, serious researchers knew the juiciest information sat in a 2-million-square-foot facility forty-five minutes away.

Flynn slumped into his seat but not before surveying his surroundings and eyeing the fellow passengers. He surmised that at least two other passengers were CIA and expected them to disappear to the archives' back entrance once they arrived. The rest looked harmless enough: an elderly lady and her husband; a school teacher; a few doctoral students, undoubtedly heading out to do research. Flynn couldn't place the last man, but concluded he was a novelist. Five minutes into the trip, Flynn's assessments proved to be spot-on, based off their conversations with one another. The two CIA agents said nothing, all but confirming Flynn's hunch.

He settled in for the ride, thumbing through his phone. Emails.

Voicemails. News. Flynn had been so consumed with the events of the past 24 hours that he was way behind on responding to emails and phone calls. Once he responded to the urgent ones, he went straight for the news.

"More Russian Sabre Rattling?" read the headline. The report detailed how the Russians were erecting new missile silos in Siberia, causing great angst in Washington. U.S. diplomats voiced concern over this move, while the Russians said it was necessary to deter any threats against their soil. Flynn rolled his eyes. *It never ends, does it?*

He decided he'd had enough world politics for today and sought out his favorite sports app to catch up on the latest NFL happenings. It was enough to occupy his time until the shuttle arrived at its destination. He watched everyone unload and head for the front entrance— except for the two men he suspected as CIA agents. They turned a corner, disappearing from view.

Once inside, Flynn put away his belongings in the lockers downstairs, taking only his burner phone with him upstairs. He went to the microfilm archive floor and called Natalie. Five minutes later, she appeared. Her piercing blue eyes and long shapely legs gave Flynn an eyeful. She tossed her thick brown hair over her shoulder as she walked toward him.

"If I didn't know any better, I would've thought you were gawking at me," Natalie said.

She gave him a friendly side hug before Flynn could even speak.

"It's good to see you, Natalie," he stammered.

"You, too."

"So, we can make small talk tonight over dinner. Whatcha got for me?"

In a hushed tone, Flynn started to divulge his protocol for passing sensitive documents over email before Natalie stopped him.

"Just air drop me the file and I'll look at it, OK?"

Flynn then relaxed and smiled. He had almost forgotten Natalie's genius idea to air drop sensitive information since it couldn't be traced back to him. He quickly uploaded the documents to her phone.

"Be back in a few minutes."

A few minutes turned into a half an hour before Natalie appeared again, this time without the bounce in her step or a smile on her face. Her face expressed a look of consternation.

"Where did you get this?" Natalie demanded.

"I told you someone gave it to me." He paused. "Is it real?"

"As far as I can tell, it is. But I'm very confused. I oversaw the JFK collection for a few years and I remember seeing that same polygraph test—with different results. Now I want to know why we have two conflicting documents."

Flynn smiled. "Good. It's always fun to have a partner in these investigations."

Natalie shook her head. "I still can't believe we have a fake document in our collection."

CHAPTER 6

SANDFORD USUALLY LOOKED FORWARD to cabinet meetings. It was his chance to give President Briggs his input, input that was normally valued. But not today. He suspected that boxing gloves—or a shiv—might be more appropriate to bring to the cabinet meeting set to begin in five minutes. Hawks on the right, doves on the left. The room would be divided along ideological party lines. President Briggs wanted to create a sense of unity by inviting leaders from both sides of the political aisle to advise him on various issues. It was one of his strengths. But when divisive issues were on the table like today, it made for a contentious meeting.

Staring at the meeting schedule on his desk, Sandford couldn't help but wonder who sent him that note. Was it a test? Was it talking about some day in the future? At first, he thought that was the case, but as he mulled it over, the message was too cryptic for such a nuanced question. It had to mean *now*. But why? The questions pinged around Briggs' brain but left him no closer to an answer. He still hadn't told a soul.

As expected, tension ruled the room during the cabinet meeting— and for good reason. The Russians had built twelve missile silos in Siberia like they were fast food chains. A once rather barren area was now being dotted by launch pads. The recent oil boom in Siberia invigorated the region known mostly for its frozen tundra, fishing industry, and prison camps. According to the Russian government, it needed to protect its precious new assets—rich oil fields. Many foreign affairs experts opined how Russia appeared to be making a play to regain its position as a world super power. Now independent from the Middle East for oil, Russia began rebuilding its army—not for protection as it claimed—but to prepare for attack. Other pundits refused to believe that Russia was stable enough to start a war with the United States. The Middle East had become a powder keg, ready to explode into war across the region. Yet defense experts never saw any of those countries as a serious threat to the United States. But Russia? The Cold War may have ended a couple of decades ago, but it wasn't a Cold War that many in the defense department now feared. They feared a real war with Russia, one looking more imminent as the country regained her footing as a global power player behind some no-nonsense leadership.

On the table in today's meeting was a proposal to build a new defense system that could handle a large volley of Russian missiles. The views of those in attendance were split evenly.

General Marshall Matthews outlined the Department of Defense's proposed missile system. The presentation included holographic images of how the system would be able to eliminate a large number of incoming missiles aimed at U.S. soil. It was quite a show and appeared to be a no-brainer to Sandford. *Just find the money in the budget and build the stupid thing. Why are we even talking about this like we might do it?* What made sense in his head apparently didn't make so much sense to everyone in the room.

Once Gen. Matthews sat down, the room erupted in furious debate. Some cabinet members were concerned about where the money would come from to build the $2-trillion system. Others posed questions about how this would look to the international community. Then there were others who thought like Sandford. The Secretary of Homeland Defense wanted it built yesterday—and he carried a significant amount of weight with the President. Despite the furor, Sandford thought there was no way President Briggs wouldn't sign off on the project.

But he didn't.

"Thank you for the presentation, General Matthews, but based on the wide variety of opinion in this room, I don't think we can go wrong either way," President Briggs said. "For now, let's table this idea and possibly revisit it if things get more heated with Russia."

Sandford perfected the art of holding his tongue in these meetings.

He was the ultimate "yes man," which was likely why he was here. But there was a time to cast off all restraint—and that time was now.

"With all due respect, Mr. President, I think that would be a mistake," Sandford said.

President Briggs cocked his head and furrowed his brow. Such dissent wasn't welcomed at this point in the meeting, particularly when everyone had a turn to speak. But Sandford didn't care, refusing to stop with a polite interruption.

"I don't know what you think you're doing, but Russia isn't building missile silos to protect their oil fields—they're building them so they can bomb us," Sandford said. "While we've sent our troops—and our money—all over the Middle East to secure oil, they've been building an oil reserve that surpasses anything we've ever done. We've got a few weeks of oil reserves. They've got a few *years*. They are poised to attack and we've got to make the gutsy call to do whatever it takes to make sure this never happens. We need a leader who has the guts to protect his people, politics be damned!"

The rare flare of emotion out of Sandford caught the entire room off guard. His impassioned plea forced several cabinet members to nod in agreement. One dissenter even muttered, "Maybe he's right."

President Briggs just glared at Sandford before restoring order to the murmuring about the room.

"I think we've heard enough from you for today. Why don't you have a seat?" President Briggs said. Nothing in his tone suggested he was about to take Sandford's advice.

And with that, the meeting moved along to the next agenda item: President Briggs' speech at the U.N. later in the week to address the hunger crisis in Central Africa.

Sandford slumped in his chair, seething over the public dressing down—and the way his advice was ignored. *Why couldn't the President see things his way? It's plain as day what is going on here. Doesn't he care about the American people?* Sandford couldn't care less about the President's speech being discussed at the moment. *They can feed all the people in Africa, but it won't matter much to the American people once missiles start flying.*

The cabinet members bantered back and forth about different ideas, but Sandford ignored them all. He started wondering—and hoping—

that the note he received in his office earlier that day was prophetic for sooner rather than later. America needed his leadership at this moment, not in a few years.

CHAPTER 7

AS MUCH AS FLYNN HATED how technology ruled his life, he appreciated how much it saved him time. But it was days like today that he loathed it. He grumbled to no one but himself that the hassle of getting a new personal phone almost wasn't worth it. *Maybe next time I won't place the phone next to the sink on the counter while I'm shaving.* It was a thought that should have occurred before he knocked it into the plugged sink. The process of getting a new one dominated his entire afternoon. He wasn't even sure it was set up right until his phone blinged with a new message.

Flynn stared at the text message on his phone and pondered his response. He hated to turn down live interviews on cable news shows, especially during prime time. His publicist would go ballistic if he found out that he opted out over dinner with a woman. But it wasn't just any woman. It was Natalie, a woman Flynn often thought would be worth laying down his demanding career for in exchange for a more normal life. *No use dreaming about the future when all I can grab is today.* He texted Natalie and asked if they could push their dinner back to 8 p.m. since he had a short interview on live television from 7:15 to 7:30. He added a frowny face on the text just to let her know he wasn't happy about the change. Seconds later she wrote back: **No problem**.

Maybe I can have the best of both worlds. He called back the *Newsmakers* show producer and agreed to go on the show. The truth is Flynn loved his job, and while snagging a catch like Natalie might be worth giving up what he got to do every day, he'd rather not. He stopped dreaming when he realized what he was doing. He hated getting ahead of himself. *Got to actually start dating first.*

As much as Flynn detested going on live television, those appearances enabled him to pursue big stories without running out of favor with his editor. Other reporters were insanely jealous of him, but he didn't care. He'd endured more than his share of snide comments while working at the agency. When fellow agents learned that Flynn's uncle worked for the agency, he became a constant subject of ridicule. All the other agents believed their hard work earned them a spot at the agency while Flynn exercised nepotism. Perhaps they were right. It was impossible to separate the two now. But sneers and snubs from co-workers were nothing new to Flynn. It only motivated him more to be better than them.

By 6 p.m., Flynn made his way to the studio to get prepped by wardrobe and makeup before getting briefed by the show's producers. The topic *Newsmakers'* producers wanted to discuss with Flynn was that of a claim from an elderly woman living in Florida. In her new book, *The Secrets That We Keep: A memoir of a Cold War house cleaning spy*, Petra Pfeiffer divulged that she worked with the CIA in a secret program named "Catomic" to spy on what U.S. officials believed were KGB operatives working out of the Russian embassy in Bonn, Germany in the 1960s. She earned $600 per month cleaning houses—and $1,500 per month by making herself available to the CIA. As the house cleaner for several KGB operatives, Pfeiffer claimed to take pictures of official documents, plant bugs, and participate in operations that granted U.S. agents access to Russian homes.

While the story gained plenty of traction in the U.S., *Newsmakers* wanted to debunk the idea that her story could be true since the CIA denied any kind of operations in Bonn during the time when Pfeiffer was supposedly an agency asset. Oddly enough to Flynn, *Newsmakers* had put Pfeiffer on the show the night before, launching her book into the top ten of bestselling books on Amazon overnight. Now, *Newsmakers* wanted to set the records straight. It's what the show did best: build up a story and then tear it down. It was the journalist equivalent of digging a ditch only to refill it. His sound bytes were sure to fill the cable news cycle for the next twenty-four hours once he outed Pfeiffer as a fraud.

Flynn told the producers that she was lying since he had firsthand knowledge that Catomic didn't start until the early 1970s. It was exactly what they wanted to hear and immediately wrote teasers for the hosts of *Page One*—the show that aired before *Newsmakers*—to read before commercial breaks in the final thirty minutes of the program.

Standing in the shadows off camera as *Newsmakers* began, Flynn looked satisfied. He detested lying, but sometimes it was necessary. And right now was one of those times. He knew all about Catomic and how the operation involved scores of civilians, both German and Americans working in Germany. Agents studied it to learn how to turn opposing agents and how to vet civilians uniquely placed to gain access to vital information. The operation qualified as espionage art form, something Flynn marveled at. And despite being expelled from the agency, he wasn't about to let Pfeiffer's loose lips hasten her demise. If he told America she was an old kook just looking for a buck after her IRA imploded, people would leave her alone. If he verified her story, she might not even live long enough to collect a royalty check.

***

AT PRECISELY 8 P.M., Flynn found a parking spot near McPherson Square and hustled across the street to his favorite restaurant, Georgia Brown's on 15th Street. As he drew nearer, the savory smells of Low Country cuisine enraptured Flynn's senses. It reminded him of home. Brunswick stew, slow-cooked pulled pork, and mustard-based barbecue sauce. The flavors nearly whisked Flynn off his feet. He hadn't lived in Charleston for a long time, but he had never forgotten the rich culture of his childhood in a place where time stood still.

As soon as Flynn opened the door, he noticed Natalie sitting in the waiting area. Draped in a stunning silvery dress, Natalie immediately gave off the impression that this was more than dinner between two friends. Her hair swirled up in a bun and her ears sporting diamond earrings, her vibe emboldened Flynn.

"Wow! Don't you look nice!" Flynn said.

Natalie feigned embarrassment before saying, "Thank you, Flynn. You don't look so bad yourself."

Flynn didn't near to hear that, but it was nice—especially as he was overly conscious of the television makeup still smeared all over his face.

The hostess seated the couple and retreated back to her post.

"You did a great job on *Newsmakers* tonight," Natalie said.

"Oh, thanks. It wasn't a big deal."

"So, tell me the truth: Was she really a spy?"

Flynn furrowed his brown and cocked his head. "Aren't you the curious one tonight?"

"Oh, stop it, James. You know I'm always curious. But I think you were lying tonight."

"How could you tell?"

"So you were lying? I knew it!" Natalie pumped her fist in excitement.

"I didn't say I was lying."

"You didn't have to. It was all over your face."

"How could you tell?"

"I may not be a trained CIA operative, but I'm trained at reading men. It lets me know if I'm an object of their affection or just an object."

"How cleverly insightful. Now I'm scared to speak."

"You've got nothing to be scared of—as long as you tell the truth."

Natalie gave Flynn a coy smile as Flynn shifted in his chair. He picked up the menu and began inspecting it closely.

"Am I making you nervous?" Natalie asked, cutting through the awkward silence.

"No. Why?"

"Don't lie to me, James," she said, giggling.

"OK, maybe a little nervous. Why do you ask?"

"Because you never need to look at the Georgia Brown's menu. You know it by heart as much as you come here. I bet you've already been here since you arrived in Washington."

He actually hadn't, but only because he was forced to go talk with detectives about Emma Taylor's death. Otherwise, lunch would have been eaten here earlier in the day.

Then Flynn's phone began buzzing. He glanced at the unknown number appearing on the screen as the phone began vibrating across the table.

"Saved by the phone." Natalie smiled. "Go ahead, answer it. I still need a minute to decide what I want to eat."

Flynn picked up his phone and answered it.

"Hello?"

"Is this James Flynn?"

"Yes, it is. May I ask who's calling?"

"My name is Sam Golden, sir. I live in Dallas, Texas, and I've got something you need to see."

"If I had a dollar for every time somebody said that to me ..." Flynn's voice trailed off, but his cynical comment didn't deter the caller.

"Look, I'm sure you get plenty of whackos calling you, but what I've got is something that warrants a trip out here."

"OK, I'm listening. What is it?"

"I just found an eight millimeter camera my father placed in a box years ago and it's got footage of JFK's assassination."

"I believe they confiscated all the cameras that were rolling in the area immediately after President Kennedy was shot."

"Well, they didn't get this one. And I think you'll be amazed at what's on it."

Flynn continued his conversation in a hushed voice. He grabbed a pen from his coat pocket and began scratching down contact information on his drink napkin before hanging up.

"So, what was that all about?" Natalie asked, apparently ready to order.

"I've got to go to Dallas tomorrow," he said. "A man just found footage of the JFK assassination that the FBI never confiscated. Apparently, it's big."

CHAPTER 8

EARLY WEDNESDAY MORNING in New York City, Ivan pressed the last wrinkle out of his white dress shirt and slipped on his coat. Security was ridiculously tight around the U.N. building every day. It became almost impenetrable when the President was scheduled to address the general assembly. Ivan looked smugly at himself in the mirror. *That's why real anarchists plot their revenge over years. You're never gonna see me coming.* He tucked his shirt in and glanced at himself once more before heading out the door.

His phone rang.

"How's our little operation coming along?" asked the voice on the other end once Ivan answered.

"Like clockwork."

"What about Flynn? Is he preoccupied?"

"Yes. His bug went dead yesterday afternoon, but I listened to everything he said. All indications were that he was moving on to other things. He especially liked the lead that we gave him with the Bay of Pigs."

"Good. We don't need him poking around any more. At least, not until we're done executing this plan on Friday."

"I understand."

Ivan hung up and reveled in his skills. Some people might label him a terrorist. It was a label Ivan found belittling. To him, the term "terrorists" represented radical ideologues. They had no purpose but to kill and destroy, all done in the name of vengeance—or, in some twisted way, God. It didn't even matter which god. Everybody seemed to follow a god that encouraged people to murder and plunder in his name. No matter the religion, some variation of God's name was invoked as a basis for an attack on other innocent people. It was disgusting really. Vengeance always proved to be such a vain pursuit. That's why Ivan loathed hearing media reports about attacks he led termed as "terrorist attacks." He wasn't exacting revenge; he had purpose to his actions. Ivan saw meaning in what he did, attempting to create a better society for everyone. So maybe there was a little collateral damage. And maybe even innocent civilians got hurt or died. What he did was for the benefit of all people—they just didn't know it yet. One day, perhaps. But certainly not now.

Twenty minutes later, Ivan arrived at Elite Catering, set to accompany his cousin, Andrei. His name meant "warrior"—and he was. Prior to moving to the United States, Andrei served in the Russian Federation army as a major. He loved his country more than anything, which is why Ivan admired him so much for leaving the motherland behind to work a thankless job in a country he loathed. Ivan realized it's what a true warrior would do.

Andrei and his deadbeat co-worker, Nelson, were scheduled to make a delivery to the U.N. A luncheon about the efforts of drought on the world's food supply necessitated Elite Catering's services. Ivan gawked at the invoice sitting next to some of the trays of food in the delivery truck before crawling beneath one of the wheeled carts. He clearly wondered how these pompous diplomats couldn't realize the irony in what they were doing. The bill was so high that it could have fed an entire village for a month. *Another reason we do what we do.*

The plan was simple: drop off the food and get Ivan in the building. Ivan handled every detail with precision. A week ago, Andrei worked with Ivan to develop a replica of the U.N.'s security clearance card as well as an ID badge for Elite Catering. The gun Ivan would be using was secured beneath the bottom of one of the carts. Since the carts always set off the metal detectors, no guard would perform a thorough search. Once inside the elevator, Andrei would allow Nelson to exit with his cart first while Andrei lingered just long enough to allow Ivan to crawl out and conceal his disassembled rifle. Ivan would continue up several floors to gain access to the balcony overlooking the general assembly and wait there until Friday.

It was a long time to wait, but it would be worth it. Nothing to do but hide and wait. Anarchy would come soon enough—and then his organization would take control.

CHAPTER 9

FLYNN GAZED OUT THE WINDOW of the DC-9 jet descending toward the Dallas-Fort Worth International Airport runway. He struggled to settle his thoughts as he had so many interesting things to think about. His burgeoning romance with Natalie. The newly discovered polygraph cover-up. And now, possible never-before-seen footage of JFK's assassination? If the latter was true, his mind might spin endlessly for days on end. It was enough to excite him about the possibility that he might be the one to discover the truth behind JFK's death. Fifty years had passed since Lee Harvey Oswald allegedly shot America's most popular President and the public was no closer to knowing the truth about what really happened. Or were they?

After Flynn secured his rental car, he headed for the address that Sam Golden gave him over the phone. He didn't make a practice of meeting people at their home, especially with all the kooks out there today. But Mr. Golden seemed harmless enough—and due to the nature of his evidence, it wasn't exactly something they could discuss and view in a public coffee shop.

While Golden claimed to live in Dallas, it was a lie. When it came to metro areas, Flynn learned most people felt such fibs were acceptable. In Georgia, nobody wants to be from Doraville. They are from Atlanta. In California, who wants to be from Culver City? Those people live in Los Angeles, no matter what the U.S. Postal Service says. And while Mr. Golden may have told Flynn that he lived in Dallas, what he really meant was Crandall.

Flynn wondered if he was in another country when he passed the city limits sign for the rural town about forty-five minutes southeast of Dallas. He noted corn stalks sticking in up people's back yards. The bedroom community of Dallas seemed to struggle with what kind of place it wanted to be—an extension of Dallas or a farming town. Only a few major restaurant chains had wormed their way into Crandall, which seemed to prefer the past over the present. White picket fences and wrap-around porches highlighted almost each house along the tree-lined streets. *It's not quite Mayberry, but it's sure trying to be.*

Sam Golden rocked in a chair on the front porch as Flynn pulled into the driveway. Apparently Sam's job could wait, whatever it was. Welcoming a big city slicker into Crandall meant no work for him.

"Are you Mr. Golden?" Flynn asked as he got out of his car.

"It's Sam. Please call me Sam," he said, lumbering down the porch steps and toward Flynn with his hand outstretched as a welcoming gesture.

They shook hands as Flynn looked around.

"Nice place you've got here," Flynn said, trying his best to be polite.

The truth was Flynn would never live in a place as run down as this. Weeds overtook the yards. More weeds spurted out of the driveway cracks. The picket fence may have been white at one time, but anybody's guess when that last was would be a legitimate one. The paint chipped off years ago, exposing the wood to the harsh Texas elements. Now, the fence simply rotted. Flynn also feared the front porch might collapse if he stepped on it at the same time as Mr. Golden. He walked behind his guest, stepping lightly and hoping for the best.

Inside, the decor of the house revolved around one thing: Texas Longhorn football. Panoramic shots of the Texas stadium. Longhorns hanging high over the room with the burnt orange logo seared into the skulls of what likely were real Longhorns at one point. A large framed portrait of Texas coach Mack Brown hoisting the national title trophy up with quarterback Vince Young. Flynn didn't even need to ask Mr. Golden how he spent his Saturdays in the fall.

Once Flynn stopped gawking, he decided to get down to business.

"So, Sam, tell me how you came across this footage of your father's?"

"Funny story, really," Mr. Golden began. "My grandson was playin' ball with one of his buddies in my backyard when they hit a baseball through the attic window. So, I went up there to fetch it for them. At first I couldn't find the ball, until I saw a box that was partially open. I opened it up to see if the ball had landed in the box—and it had. But then I saw this home movie camera I remember my dad using when we were all little. I just couldn't remember him using it anymore at some point. I had no idea what caused my father to stop filming us, but he did.

"Anyway, I set up the projector I found in this box and put the reel on. And that's when I found the footage that I'm about to show you. You better be sitting down when I show it."

Flynn could tell this wasn't dramatic hyperbole from his guest.

Mr. Golden darkened the room and fired up the projector. It whirred and wheezed until it gathered speed and began to show the images more clearly.

The brisk November morning started with Mr. Golden and his brothers loading into the family station wagon. The camera captured a few shots of the brothers goofing off in the car before the scene shifted suddenly to Elm Street in downtown Dallas, where thousands of adoring citizens waved and cheered for the President. Then the shots rang out.

Mr. Golden's father dove to the ground, yelling at his boys and his wife to do the same. While the camera was still running, the lens fell aiming toward a culvert about ten feet away. Though it was difficult to make out at first, the camera focused on a dark-skinned man clutching a gun in the culvert. He suddenly disappeared from view moments before the camera was hastily whisked away and turned off.

Flynn knew the area well, including the exact location of that culvert. Several conspiracy theories floated around about a second gunman on the grass knoll. But the hard core conspiracy theorists knew of a much more plausible place for the gunman to be: hiding in the culvert at street level.

However, Flynn gasped when the evidence revealed something far more sinister and unbelievable than he could ever imagine.

"Is everything OK, Mr. Flynn?" Mr. Golden asked.

"Yeah, I think so."

"Well, what is it?"

"It's impossible—but I think I know the man who shot JFK."

CHAPTER 10

GERALD SANDFORD COULD HARDLY pay attention to his wife's ramblings about the latest Capitol Hill gossip. Not that he didn't like to hear the latest scoop over which politician was the latest to be outed by the Fly on the Wall blog. Any rumor spread in Washington about a political figure was sure to be detailed by the blog's anonymous writer. Most politicians suspected that one person couldn't be so well connected to hear all these rumors and that it must be a team of writers. Several congressmen suspected their staffers participated in either writing or passing along the often damning information. What appeared on front pages of newspapers across the nation likely appeared on the Fly on the Wall blog first. Most evenings, Sandford would be riveted as he listened to his wife, Sarah, recount what she read, particularly when it happened to one of his political foes. But not tonight.

As Sarah babbled on about who got caught with their pants down, Sandford gazed across the room at nothing in particular. The contentious cabinet meeting the day before still bothered him. He wished for a simpler time, perhaps a time when leading a nation wasn't so complicated. Now opinions flowed freely from every hack with Internet access, making it more difficult to control delicate situations. The World Wide Web set back government propaganda five hundred years. Instead of controlling the press, the press controlled the government. All they had to do was write or broadcast any idea they ginned up and proffered it as "what most Americans believe" or "what most Americans want." *If only most Americans knew what really went on. Not many have the stomach to do what it takes to lead.*

Sandford watched with dismay as his longtime friend, President Briggs, fell victim to this new game of the tail wagging the dog. All his decisions appeared to be based on the latest poll results. Not that he needed to worry about them since he was already into his second term. But Briggs appeared more concerned about his public image than doing the right thing. Sandford had been at this long enough to know the public doesn't always know what's best. They only know what the media tells them, which is an entity with its own agenda. At least weak-stomached presidents in the past were led around by deep-pocketed donors instead of the media—and public polls.

The more Sandford thought about it, the angrier he got. How could he let this happen to the country he loved so much? If he were president, then he'd be doing his job, protecting the American people and upholding the Constitution. He wouldn't be caught dead even looking at polling numbers. As he mulled what to do to get President Briggs to reconsider, the thoughts that went through his mind embarrassed him. Some of them were criminal, like blackmail. He had more than enough dirt on President Briggs to sink him in one fell swoop. But that was his nuclear option. Good statesmanship required a different type of persuasion, one that appealed to the best nature in someone. Sandford just didn't know if that nature even still dwelled in the President's mind. He determined to think of something. And if he didn't, he would hope that cryptic message he received would ring true any day now.

Sandford didn't hear his wife until she realized he wasn't engaged in her story about the congressman from North Dakota who got a D.U.I. and was also charged with possession of moonshine.

"Gerald? Gerald?" Sarah asked. "Are you listening to me?"

He snapped out of his stupor.

"Oh, no, I'm sorry, honey. I've got a lot on my mind these days. What were you saying?"

"Never mind. Just finish up so I can get us dessert."

Sandford stared at his plate. He'd hardly eaten a bite of his wife's baked chicken, one of his favorites.

Then his phone rang, prompting him to get up from the table to take the call. The number was blocked. He went into his office and shut the door.

"This is Sandford."

"Is this Vice President Gerald Sandford?"

Sandford struggled to place the accent. It sounded Eastern European, but he couldn't be certain.

"Yes, it is. With whom am I speaking?"

"That's not important. What's important is that I tell you something about your daughter. I know who took her—and so does the Russian government."

"What do you mean 'took her'? She was killed sixteen years ago."

"Is that what they told you? Well, don't believe everything you hear from the Russian government. They take their time and strike when you least expect it."

"Who is this?" Sandford demanded, his voice rising.

"Just remember what I told you: When you become President..."

"Hey. Who are you —-"

The caller hung up, leaving Sandford alone to decipher what it all meant. If anything, it picked at an old wound, the wound that became the driving force for Sandford's political ambition. He wanted justice for his daughter's death. But if the caller was to be believed, Sydney wasn't dead after all. All his buttons were being pushed and he couldn't handle it.

Sarah knocked on the door and poked her head in.

"Is everything OK, Gerald? Who was that?"

"I don't know. Somebody's messing with me. It's nothing." Sandford slumped into the chair behind his desk.

"OK, I'm about to bring out dessert."

"Honey, I've got to be honest—I'm not really hungry right now. Can you save me some for later?"

"Sure thing," she said as she closed the door behind him, leaving him alone in the office.

Sandford buried his head in his hands and let out an exasperated sigh. He didn't know what to believe. He especially didn't like being toyed with. But getting worked up was no way to govern. *You rule with your head, not your heart*, Sandford's father told him when he first got elected to represent his home state of Tennessee as a representative. At the moment neither seemed sufficient.

He placed a call to his office and asked a staffer to get the NSA to track the most recent call placed to his cell phone. He waited in silence before a quick response came back: they couldn't trace it—neither the phone's owner nor the location.

Sandford decided he needed a drink, a strong drink. Vodka would suffice. *At least there's one thing good to come out of that godforsaken country.* Sandford slammed the drink down and poured himself another. He needed to think about what his first move would be as President.

CHAPTER 11

FLYNN STILL FELT LIKE he was groping in the dark, trying desperately to make sense of the shards of evidence he had collected. It was one thing to identify the shooter—the real shooter in the JFK assassination plot. It was another to figure out whom he was working for. By his estimation, Flynn solved the easy part. The question everybody wanted answered still clung to his back like a 400-pound gorilla.

Navigating afternoon traffic in Dallas was not one of the more glamorous parts of the job. After visiting Sam Golden in Crandall, Flynn returned to Dallas proper for another meeting he'd delayed for several weeks. He received a call from a man named Stephen Moore who had some documents he wanted to give to Flynn—but it had to be in person. He asked Mr. Moore to wait patiently until he could get there. Fortunately, the invitation to see Sam Golden's video gave Flynn the opportunity to make it a two-for-one trip, something that would make those finance people at *The National* happy.

Flynn also wanted to make Theresa happy, which is why he recorded a playback of Sam Golden's footage of the shooter hidden in the culvert. It took all of three minutes, after he emailed the footage to his editor, for her to call him back.

"Are you serious? Is this for real?" Theresa asked.

"You know me. I always air on the side of caution and cynicism. But if this is a hoax, it's one elaborate one. Just get an expert to compare it with official television footage. It shouldn't be hard to prove or disprove."

"But we have no idea that the man in the culvert actually fired his weapon."

"I'm not concerned with whether he fired his weapon or not. I want to know who he is."

"Do you have any idea of who he might be?"

"Strangely enough—yes. But it's going to take some time to verify who he is."

"Got any friends left at the CIA who can help out?"

"I've still got a few friends there, but this is not something I want to transmit to them and put into their database as coming from me. Just give me some time. I'll see what I can come up with."

"Take all the time you need. You know this might be bigger than Watergate."

"Maybe. Depends on who was really behind it all—the only question that needs to be answered at this point."

"Just keep me posted, OK?"

Flynn bid his editor a good afternoon before hanging up and turning his full attention back to the road. But it didn't stay there for long before his mind began to drift. *How could this be possible? It doesn't make sense.*

A half hour later, Flynn arrived at Mr. Moore's residence. He remained in the car for a moment to ponder what might be next as he stared at the manicured yard in the center of this upper-middle-class neighborhood. The week's events sent Flynn's mind spinning as he worked through the evidence to find the shred of truth that would unravel the lie sold to the American public. Could Mr. Moore's documents shed more light on the JFK assassination conspiracy or simply lead to more questions? Flynn hoped his victorious battle against Dallas' afternoon traffic would yield a positive result for the case. He hated more questions in a conspiracy this old.

Flynn knocked on the black door of the brick ranch house and waited. The door creaked open, revealing a gentleman who appeared to be somewhere around eighty years old. The thin splotches of white hair dotting his otherwise bald head and his slightly hunched back alerted Flynn that his host had a few stories to tell. Yet there was only one that interested him.

Mr. Moore welcomed Flynn and showed him to the den where the two settled into plush chairs. They made small talk for a few minutes before addressing the main reason for their meeting.

"So, Mr. Moore, what documents did your brother give you that were so important you had to give them to me in person?" Flynn asked.

Mr. Moore chuckled, which quickly turned into a gravely cough. Upon regaining his composure, Mr. Moore answered him.

"I'm a big fan and I wanted to meet you in person," Mr. Moore said.

"Seriously?" Flynn asked, starting to seethe beneath his breath.

"Absolutely. But that's not the only reason I wanted to see you in person. It has to do with the nature of these documents, documents that my brother said were for your eyes only."

Flynn sighed.

"Look, if I don't have your permission to share these with the public when I go to write a story—if these documents are even newsworthy—then this is just a waste of time for both of us."

Flynn abruptly stood up to leave.

"Now, now, Mr. Flynn. I didn't say you couldn't share the information. Only the documents can't be broadcast or shown to anyone. However, he was a big fan of yours too and made a short video for you to watch. He never said anything about not showing it to anyone."

With that last sentence, Mr. Moore gave Flynn a wink and turned on the television with the video apparently already cued up.

The video started with an introduction by Mr. Moore's brother, who surprisingly was only ten days away from dying. He was rather lucid and appeared in good spirits as he began talking.

> Hi, Mr. Flynn. My name is James Moore, but you likely know me as J. Walton Moore, a CIA agent based here in Dallas in the 1960s. As I near death, I think it's important that the world know the truth about cover stories I told when deposed by the Warren Commission and the House Select Committee on Assassinations.
>
> I first met George de Mohrenschildt at a charity event in Dallas in early 1962. At the time, he believed it was a

chance meeting, but it was nothing of the sort. I had been tasked by the Deputy Director of Plans, Mr. Richard Helms, to make contact with Mr. de Mohrenschildt and deploy him as an asset for Central Intelligence. I was unsure the extent of Mr. Helm's plans for our new asset. However, I was instructed to introduce him to Lee Harvey Oswald when he and his wife first moved to Dallas in the spring of 1963.

The agency helped arrange for Mr. de Mohrenschildt to win a government contract with Haiti, deploying him there with the express purpose of gathering intel on the movements of Francois Duvalier's relatively new government. Anybody cozying up to Fidel Castro in those days came under intense scrutiny from the agency.

Just before Mr. de Mohrenschildt moved to Haiti in June of 1963, I met with him and Helms in Washington to go over protocol for delivering intelligence. Mr. de Mohrenschildt moved away and never reported much of anything until he returned to the United States in 1967.

Officially, Mr. de Mohrenschildt never met Oswald again. That's agency speak for "yes they did meet, but I'm not going to tell you about it." In mid September, Mr. de Mohrenschildt took a trip to Mexico City and just so happened to run into Lee Harvey Oswald. I have no idea what they discussed, but I do know other more well known assassins were rumored to be present at the meeting.

Ultimately, because of Mr. de Mohrenschildt's detailed knowledge of the events and activities that happened around the President's assassination, the CIA resurrected Project Artichoke to keep him from talking. Under the influence of a special cocktail of drugs, Mr. de Mohrenschildt took his own life before he could speak with the House Select Committee on Assassinations in 1977.

This is not something I'm proud of, but I couldn't go to my grave without telling the truth, something Mr. de Mohrenschildt never had the opportunity to do himself.

Thank you for your time.

The screen faded to black, but Flynn, mouth agape, still stared at it. It was easily the most powerful admission he had ever seen or heard. Shocking Flynn was not easy to do. He carried more secrets than he ever had time to divulge, some of which could start wars between nations. But this? This deathbed confession supplanted anything at the top of his list for jaw-dropping moments.

"Has anyone else seen this?" Flynn asked.

"Nope. And I was under specific instructions to show it to you first," Mr. Moore said. "My brother was hoping that maybe you'd be able to use this during one of your television appearances when you talked about it. He even made a copy for you."

Mr. Moore shoved a DVD into Flynn's hands along with a written transcript and some other background information that he felt might come in handy while writing his story.

Flynn thanked Mr. Moore but remained in a daze, his brain whirring over the implications of what he just heard.

"Do you know what this means?" Flynn asked.

"Not much other than the CIA killed a man," Mr. Moore answered. "You really think that's a big deal."

"Well, it's much more than that. Conspiracy theorists have long since believed that the CIA had a hand in killing JFK. Now we've got an agent admitting that the CIA coerced a man to kill himself before he could share any information about JFK's assassination."

"I thought everyone believed that, Mr. Flynn," Mr. Moore replied. "The bigger questions are who else was behind it and why."

Mr. Moore's response deflated any excitement Flynn had over the deathbed admission. He still found it significant—a witness testimony confirming that the CIA really was involved in JFK's assassination plot. Or at the very least, had knowledge that something was happening. Mr. Moore may not have been impressed, but Flynn trusted his gut that this story was huge, the biggest he'd ever covered. He trusted his editor would agree with him along with the cable news shows. This had "book deal" written all over it.

Despite his exuberance, Mr. Moore was right. The admission did nothing more that confirm suspicions and raise old questions again. Why would the CIA want JFK dead? Was it over his reluctance to engage in the Vietnam conflict? Were they scared he would divulge important state secrets during one of his trysts with a foreign model posing as a spy? Or was Lyndon B. Johnson pulling the CIA's strings to find his way to the White House in a more prominent position?

The *why* was nearly as interesting as the *who* on a mystery that was now a half century old. Everyone believed the Warren Report was flawed. Now Flynn had proof.

He needed to pull on one more thread, one he hoped would unravel these secrets with the ever-elusive smoking gun.

CHAPTER 12

FLYNN SAT IN HIS CAR outside Mr. Moore's house for a few minutes. He needed to calm down and think. Up until now, every new shred of evidence Flynn collected came from private citizens divulging some family secret. The web of lies proved the CIA's culture of deceit still thrived. But the conscience of a few people weighed heavily upon them, so much so that they had to get the truth out there.

The fact that it took a half a century for these confessions and pieces of evidence to start coming out led Flynn to believe that the job of providing information and misinformation by the CIA was intentional. They wanted the media and the public to believe that almost anyone associated with JFK had motive to forcibly remove him from office. Over the years, Flynn met scores of people with a variety of theories. The mob did it. J. Edgar Hoover did it. LBJ did it. Russia did it. Cuba did it. Some people even suspected shipping magnate Aristotle Onassis did it. The last one was Flynn's personal favorite, even though it was outlandish. The rumor was Kennedy was about to enact a crippling tax to the foreign import industry in the U.S., which would all but ruin Onassis. Yet Flynn liked it because if it were true, Onassis not only offed Kennedy but married his widow Jacqueline as well. The ultimate "up yours." But the people who believed that conspiracy were a special kind of crazy, the kind Flynn avoided at all costs.

Ultimately, the plan of leaked information and misinformation achieved the CIA's desired result. While some people still suspect the agency's role in JFK's assassination plot, there were far more plausible—and titillating—theories that abounded.

Flynn liked the direction of his investigation thus far, particularly since it centered around de Mohrenschildt. Easily Flynn's favorite suspect, de Mohrenschildt led a colorful life that boarded on the unbelievable if not fanciful. Born into a wealthy shipping family in Russia in 1911, de Mohrenschildt found his silver-spoon life turned upside down when his father was imprisoned during the Bolshevik Revolution. But in 1921, his father managed to escape a prison camp in Siberia, leading his family to freedom in Poland. As a young man, he spent time all over Europe, even claiming to become involved in a Nazi plot to assassinate Joseph Stalin.

In 1938, de Mohrenschildt came to the U.S., seeking his fame and fortune—at least, that's what he told everyone. From the moment he stepped on U.S. soil, the FBI began compiling a detailed dossier of his movements and liaisons. Long suspected as a Nazi spy, then later, KGB, de Mohrenschildt lived his life under the watchful auspices of American spies. Yet it didn't deter him from growing his network of questionable contacts in the U.S. and abroad. In the meantime, de Mohrenschildt— ever the opportunist—built a sizeable wealth by preying on wealthy widows. It wasn't until he married his fourth wife that he actually found a woman he deemed worth keeping, albeit a rocky marriage that even included a secret divorce while the couple continued living together.

Flynn loved the delicious irony over a Russian national and suspected Nazi spy being turned and deployed as an asset by the CIA. Yet he scratched his head over how anyone could conceive that de Mohrenschildt could be trustworthy. Weren't his self-serving actions as obvious to the agency then when it approached de Mohrenschildt about becoming an asset as they were now, fifty years later? It befuddled Flynn how they could miss such glaring problems.

Of all Flynn's personal conspiracy theories regarding the JFK assassination, the idea that George de Mohrenschildt was pulling the strings was among the most intriguing, and quite plausible. The CIA even arranged a meeting between him and Lee Harvey Oswald when the Oswalds moved to Dallas. And the iconic picture of Oswald holding a rifle? It was de Mohrenschildt behind the camera that day. *Could this guy have played the CIA? Or was this the CIA's plan all along?* What was once a far-fetched idea seemed entirely plausible in light of J. Walton Moore's deathbed confession. But without de Mohrenschildt to confirm or deny anything, it was still just a theory, one that still needed more legs to stand on. It was just like the CIA wanted it.

Several years ago, Flynn wrote a story about de Mohrenschildt for *The National.* It looked at his life and his role in some of the most significant moments in world history as a supposed innocent bystander. Yet Flynn contended that was far from the truth. He painted de Mohrenschildt as a slimy mercenary on the open espionage market, ready to flip for whoever was willing to pay for it. He remembered de Mohrenschildt's daughter, Alexei, wasn't very happy about it. Fortunately, she was a drunk and likely didn't remember the piece. In hindsight, Flynn realized he didn't have to be so harsh in the stance he took against his favorite alleged conspirator. Hopefully, Alexei had forgiven him—or was too drunk to remember who he was.

He needed to pay her a visit.

***

FLYNN WOKE UP THURSDAY MORNING in his hotel room with one surprising thing on his mind: Natalie. He couldn't wait to escape Dallas and get back to Washington to see her. While in the gaudy Texas metropolis, Flynn had seen enough bleached blonde hair to last him another five years or so. And if he saw another obnoxious car commercial with a guy wearing a big white hat and shouting at him at the top of his lungs, he just might take a flying leap out of his hotel room. The fact that his room was on the first floor of the Hilton downtown meant it would only be a symbolic gesture. *Just hang in there for a few more hours and you'll get to see Natalie soon enough.* That thought alone gave Flynn the desire to endure what might be a disastrous morning meeting.

And while Flynn may have dreaded staying there any longer and possibly facing the wrath of a sober Alexei de Mohrenschildt, it was an important meeting with tremendous potential.

When Flynn called Alexei the night before, she gave him a different address than the one he had in his contact list. She had recently moved to a much larger home. Flynn found that odd since Alexei was a widowed woman in her mid-60s. *Why would she need a bigger home?* Then Flynn dismissed the thought, concurring that *everything really is bigger in Texas.* The two-story brick home sat inside a gated community. More pristine manicured yards. For the few driveways that held cars, it looked like a luxury used car lot—with Mercedes, BMW, and Lexus well represented. *She's moving up in the world. Not bad for a drunk.*

Flynn pressed the doorbell and waited for Alexei to answer. She never took her husband's last name, proud of her past and her father— no matter what people thought about him. When Flynn saw her, he was taken aback by her appearance. Instead of unkempt hair and a bathrobe, Alexei wore a tight-fitting black leather skirt and a white blouse. Her brown hair looked much healthier, cropped tightly around her shoulders. It was almost as if she were a different person.

She welcomed him into her home and led him to a solarium just off the main entryway inside the house.

"It's good to see you, Ms. de Mohrenschildt," Flynn said. "Thank you for taking the time to talk with me."

"My pleasure," she said. "What can I do for you?"

"Well, I came here today to ask you a few questions and to show you something."

"What do you want to show me?"

"I have a DVD of a CIA operative admitting on his deathbed that the government used a cocktail of drugs to coerce your father to shoot himself."

Flynn eyed her cautiously, unsure of how she might react. Surprisingly, she remained cold.

"I'll save us both some time and pass on watching it, Mr. Flynn. I knew that a long time ago."

"Really?"

"Well, I figured the U.S. government didn't give our family large sums of money each month just because my dad was a good person. What did you think? That I bought this house on my good looks," she said. Then she paused briefly before speaking again. "Don't answer that last question."

Flynn smiled. He enjoyed the sober Alexei. Her wit was sharp, something absent in their last meeting. Maybe this time she could remember something of value.

"So what did you want to ask me?" she said.

"Do you remember going on any trips with your father and him meeting any suspicious people?"

"Everyone who met with my father was suspicious. When you work with spies and thieves, nobody shows up wearing a frock, if you know what I mean."

"Well, it's come to light that the CIA used your father to help orchestrate JFK's assassination. But based on some other information I've found, I have a theory that he used the CIA as a cover and worked with some other organizations first. Would you be able to help me with any information here?"

Alexei tilted her head and pursed her lips before finally speaking.

"Trying to single one out is next to impossible. My father would've sold his soul to both Jesus and the Devil if he could've figured out a way to swindle both of them into buying it at the same time."

"Do you remember where the people were from?"

"Haiti, Germany, France, Yugoslavia, Cuba, Mexico—you name it, my father was meeting officials from all these countries."

"What about the Russians?"

"Oh, yes, he met with several Russians—" Alexei then paused. "But they weren't with the Russian government. It was a funny Russian name. Oh, what was it?"

Flynn sat there helpless, praying that of all the brain cells Alexei killed while drinking for years that she hadn't killed the ones carrying that name.

"I can't remember. Something like Cuckoo Clocks or Kooky Cods. No, that's no it."

Flynn patiently awaited the answer to find its way to Alexei's tongue.

"Kuklovod! That's it—the Kuklovod. He was always meeting with them. Especially when we lived in Haiti. I only remember that because he would say their name in Russian since we didn't speak it. But I just always started giggling whenever I heard it."

She smiled at the fond memory, unaware of its implications.

"Do you know anything else about them?"

"Not much—but I do know they left us a lot of money. And I

mean a *lot* of money."

"Did your father ever talk about what it was for?"

"No. He never spoke of them at all once we left Haiti and returned to the states."

Flynn asked Alexei a few more questions, but it didn't go anywhere. And within ten minutes, Flynn concluded there was no more information to extract from his gracious host. She showed him to the door.

Once inside his car, Flynn dialed one of his few remaining friends at the CIA, Todd Osborne. They spent a few minutes catching up on personal life details before Flynn finally got around to the nature of his call.

"So, I've got a question for you. Have you ever heard of the Kuklovod?"

Osborne said nothing.

"Osborne? Are you there?"

More silence.

"Osborne?"

Finally, Osborne spoke. "Yeah, I'm here. I'm just in shock, that's all."

"About what? What can you tell me about the Kuklovod?"

"Honestly, I can't tell you much—but I can tell you that they were once one of the most formidable terrorist groups in the world. Their operatives were better than ours, if truth be told."

"Is that all?"

"One last thing: if you're following a lead on a story that points to them, stop right now. You don't want to get mixed up with them."

Flynn thanked Osborne for the information and hung up.

He pumped his fist in the car as he drove toward the airport. He wasn't about to stop now, no matter how dangerous Osborne claimed they were. No journalist stops this short of the finish line. He was prepared, no matter what the cost.

Yet Flynn had no idea just how costly it could be.

CHAPTER 13

IVAN LOOKED AT HIS WATCH. It was noon on Thursday. *Just over 24 hours down and just over 24 hours to go. By two o'clock tomorrow, it will all be over.* He smiled at the thought.

Believing in a cause—doing something that mattered with his life—meant doing unpleasant things at times. This was one of those times. His back ached from sitting in a cramped position. After spending months studying the schematics of the U.N.'s general assembly hall, he knew there was only one place he could hide and not be seen by the Secret Service's obligatory sweep of the building. For years, his organization—the Kuklovod—knew the President's Secret Service created a false sense of security. They served more as a deterrent for undisciplined terrorists than a true line of defense. While imposing, the Secret Service was far from infallible, a point he was going to prove very soon when the President addressed the U.N.

The worst part of his hiding spot high above the general assembly meeting hall was that he could only move minimally for just over two days. With a couple of bottles of water jammed into his coat pockets, Ivan felt even more restricted by the Elite Catering uniform. A dark jacket, white dress shirt and black slacks propagated the idea that he was there to serve food and nothing else. It was uncomfortable but necessary for when impending chaos reigned in the building. He would walk out and disappear into the turbulent city streets.

With his phone in one coat pocket and his Bluetooth earpiece securely fastened, Ivan placed a call. He wanted to check in to let everyone know the plan was running smoothly.

"What's Flynn up to?" the man on the other end of the line asked.

"As far as we can tell, nothing that would derail us from our plan. We haven't been able to listen in on his calls, but I got a report that he flew to Dallas earlier this week and is still there."

"And that doesn't concern you?"

"No. Should it?"

"Dallas is home to many secrets."

"And most of them are buried now."

"Don't be so confident. I'll dispatch another operative to track him. We don't want to get surprised by anything he does."

"Just relax. You'll get what you want soon enough."

"Do what you're supposed to do and get out of there. We have plenty of work to do here yet."

Ivan knew he was right. Removing President Briggs solved nothing in and of itself. Starting a world war wasn't easy. The fuse needed to be set ever so delicately. The reward needed to outweigh the risk. The players needed to have sufficient motivation to cast off all restraint.

The poor little people of the United States, thinking they live in such a safe place. They'll never see us coming.

For the plan to be a guaranteed success, Ivan needed to kill President Briggs. It was worth the momentary discomfort. It would all be over soon enough.

CHAPTER 14

FLYNN CHECKED HIS VOICE MESSAGES on the way to the airport. Theresa left a message telling Flynn she needed him in New York City on Friday to cover the President's speech at the U.N. about the growing famine crisis in Central Africa. Apparently not one but two staff writers had come down with a nasty illness that required the change. Theresa sounded apologetic in her message, but it didn't change the fact that Flynn would have to put his investigation on hold and reroute his flight. *Oh, boy, I get to partake in the joys of airline customer service!*

There was also a message from Natalie. She said she found something very interesting that might make for a good story. In an attempt to stimulate Flynn's interest, Natalie didn't reveal any of the details or the nature of her findings. She knew a cryptic message would garner a return phone call. Flynn laughed as he deleted her message. He knew she just wanted to talk and wondered if she'd even found anything at all.

Still twenty minutes out from the airport, Flynn tuned into one of Dallas' 24-hour news radio stations to catch up on what was happening in the present. Spending all your time living in the past can lead to an unhealthy view on life. So can spending all your time investigating conspiracy theories. Both practices took their toll on Flynn. If his mother were still alive, Flynn doubted he would trust her. She would've probably been some double-agent spy grooming him to gather some highly sensitive intel so she could sell it to the highest bidder. Somehow he doubted she would've been making him peanut butter and jelly sandwiches and taking him to school every day.

Yet it was his cynicism and suspicion that made him a rock star in his field. No story was too unbelievable, nor was it ever believable on its surface. Lies weave the tapestry of a world people *want* to live in, not a world they *actually* live in. Sometimes lies are told to them; other times people lie to themselves. Ultimately, the truth ends up hidden in a dense fog of deceit. Just understanding the level of dishonesty in the world was enough to make any man cynical. But it was that understanding that also drove Flynn to relentlessly pursue the truth until he'd exposed every lie. His cynicism served him well, yet he hoped it wouldn't destroy him either. He wanted to believe every word out of Natalie's mouth, but he just knew better. People rarely say what they mean—that's what he learned in his CIA training on understanding body language and the art of deciphering the truth. It was a class that served as the foundation for gathering intelligence and determining its usefulness, not to mention its authenticity. As difficult as it might be to gather enough plausible evidence to reveal the truth about who ordered the assassination of JFK and why, Flynn possessed the resolve necessary to bring it to light.

Flynn turned his attention back to the radio, listening intently to a report about the growing tensions between the U.S. and Russia. *What year is this? 1984?* He struggled to believe that after all the goodwill engendered between the two super powers over the past twenty years that suddenly they would go right back to sabre rattling with threatening rhetoric.

Russia scared Flynn like no other country could. While serving as a CIA operative, Flynn went behind the curtain to learn about the terrible atrocities being committed by ruthless leaders all over the world. Some of the tyrants in Africa even possessed chemical weapons. But the CIA ignored them, knowing Africa had more to lose by using a chemical weapon against the U.S.—if they even had a delivery method. The CIA didn't hesitate to turn a blind eye to such activity. They wanted plausible deniability if somehow one of these leaders ever figured out a way to deploy a chemical weapon in the U.S. But that was not the case for Russia. Threats emanating out of Russia were taken seriously. It's one thing to dismiss a threatening country with a disorganized, untrained, and ill-equipped army and no air or naval support. But Russia is in far better shape to carry through on a threat. What the CIA—and everyone in the Department of Defense—feared were the ideological leaders within the Russian government. If Russian leaders ever felt they could unequivocally launch an attack on the U.S. leading to its demise and conquer, they would do it. And that's why Flynn shuddered when he heard the news reports.

Fortunately, President Briggs was a dove, determined to exhaust all diplomatic efforts rather than join in a refrain of threats. Yet the President's advisors seemed happy to talk tough through the media. It made Flynn uneasy about the situation and what might happen should one pro-war advisor make an impassioned plea for the use of force on Russia. All someone had to do was light the fuse.

Flynn's phone buzzed, snapping him out of all his dark "what if" scenarios. It was Osborne. He had been expecting his call. Flynn called The Liaison in Washington and asked if they could pull a good screen shot of him and the man who approached him with a package earlier in the week. With the estimated time and location of their meeting, it was easy. The security guard emailed the image to Flynn's phone—The Liaison staff would do anything for one of their favorite customers. Flynn then forwarded the image along to Osborne to get an ID on the mystery man. Hopefully, Osborne had an answer for him.

"OK, I don't know what you're doing, Flynn, but you've got to seriously consider stopping," Osborne pleaded.

"So you're saying I'm on to something?"

"I'm not saying you're onto something, but I am saying they're on to you."

"Who?"

"The Kuklovod."

"That guy works for the Kuklovod?"

"Not only does he work for them, but he's also their top assassin, according to intelligence reports. They don't call him Ivan the Terrible for no reason."

"What does he want with me?"

"He probably doesn't want you poking your nose into their business. It's best you lay low for a while so you don't suffer the same fate as that poor girl you met with."

"What am I doing that's making them so nervous?"

"That's not a question I can answer, Flynn. You have to ask yourself that and determine what's going on here. Over the past few years, the Kuklovod remained inactive according to our sources. If they were doing anything, it wasn't on our radar. But somehow you've gotten on theirs."

Flynn lied. "I just don't know what would make them come after me."

"Just be careful, OK?"

Flynn agreed to be more careful before hanging up. The truth was he had no such plans. His ruthless pursuit of the truth didn't stop with some possible assassin trying to throw him off the trail. Now was the time to press on. He could take care of himself. *Who does Osborne think I am? Some weak-kneed journalist?* Pulling the shroud off conspiracies took determination. Being trained to kill another man with your bare hands didn't hurt either. Flynn hoped it wouldn't come to that, but he would be ready if it did.

CHAPTER 15

GERALD SANDFORD EYED THE PICTURE on his screen, struggling with which emotion to unleash. He could cry or shove his fist through the wall. Either response would be deemed appropriate given the circumstances of the image staring back at him.

It was Sydney with today's newspaper.

The fact that the newspaper she held was *The Pravda* made Sandford angry. For a long time, he believed he had lost his daughter because of the Russian government's ineffectiveness to ward off Chechnyan rebels. Now he wondered if he had simply lost sixteen years because of their ineptitude. Or maybe Russia planned this all along, waiting for the right time to use his daughter as leverage. If it was the latter, they had severely underestimated him.

While the American government had a long-standing policy of not dealing with terrorists, Sandford scoffed at that clumsy language proffered by White House spokespeople. "I will deal with terrorists," Sandford used to tell his constituents. "I'll deal with them in ways that will make them regret ever raising a finger against our great nation." It was a line that went over well, solidifying his position as a politician who was serious about protecting the American people. In all his years in office, Sandford never actually had a chance to mete out his tough talk on terrorists. But now he might. He just needed to figure out who the real terrorists were: the rebels or the Russian government. Someone was going to pay.

Sandford forwarded the image from his phone to his email account.

He first needed verification that the image was authentic. Then he needed to know where it came from. And he needed it all done off book. Sandford danced uncomfortably close to the line that divided moral from immoral, ethical from unethical, legal from illegal. He didn't go there often, but he didn't have to think twice when it came to his daughter's life. *Anybody would do what I'm doing.* He reasoned away his questionable behavior that would surely get a closer look from some Senate ethics committee—if they ever found out. However, Sandford took the necessary precaution to ensure they never would.

There was only one person he trusted at the CIA: Todd Osborne. Sydney and Todd were friends in college, attending Princeton at the same time. One spring break, Sydney brought Osborne to their family beach house in Naples, Florida. She had spoken of him, but only in terms of a platonic friendship. It didn't take Sandford long to realize why he had been invited: Osborne wanted her friend's Senator father to help him get a job with the CIA. At the time, majoring in Russian didn't make him a likely candidate on his own merit, but Sandford gladly pulled some strings. But he did it with the condition that Osborne would be his guy in the agency.

It took Osborne a while to move up the CIA's security clearance level to become useful to Sandford. But once he did, Sandford didn't mind asking for favors. It had been a while since he asked for one, but he was sure Osborne would oblige his request. Though Osborne had played coy when asked about the extent of his relationship with Sydney, Sandford could tell the young man had been fond of his daughter.

Sandford dialed Osborne's number. After a few minutes of small talk, Sandford made the purpose of his call clear.

"Look, Todd. I need your help on something here."

"Sure, Mr. Sandford. What do you need?"

"I need something done off book—and it has to do with Sydney."

"Sydney? I thought she died years ago. Are you saying she is still alive?"

"Maybe. That's what I need you to verify for me. I'm going to send a picture over to you and I need you to get this done without this image getting into the CIA system—or anyone else finding out her identity. If it's real, it's going to dictate some decisions I need to make."

"I understand, Mr. Sandford. I'll handle the matter with complete discretion."

Osborne gave the Vice President an email account that couldn't be easily traced back to him before vowing to get a quick answer.

***

WHEN THE WHEELS TOUCHED DOWN at JFK Airport in New York, Flynn pulled out his phone and began reviewing his itinerary for the next day. Theresa had her assistant forward him a schedule that was already waiting in his inbox. He couldn't believe the rigorous demands. In the morning, he was set to interview an environmentalist about a simple water purification system his organization was installing throughout Africa. Theresa wanted him to file a short piece for *The National*'s blog before attending the President's speech on Central Africa's famine at the U.N. in the afternoon. The link between the two made sense to Theresa. Flynn was just irked that his day was so packed. *We'll blow ourselves up before we ever save the earth.* No one ever accused Flynn of being an optimist.

He called the office to check in and let them know that he would be where they asked him to be. Then he dialed Natalie's number, hoping to catch her before she left the office for the day. She answered.

"So, I guess we're off for tonight?" Natalie said.

"Unfortunately, yes. I've got a busy day ahead tomorrow. Maybe I can catch a train to Washington this weekend."

Natalie perked up.

"I like that idea. What did you have in mind?"

"Not sure yet, but I'll think of something."

"You always do—but it better be good."

Flynn laughed and promised it would be. *I have no idea what to do for fun in Washington. Who am I kidding?*

He then collected his carry-on and exited the plane.

Suddenly, he felt his burner phone buzzing. *Who could this be?* The number was blocked.

He answered. "Hello?"

"Be careful what you do, Mr. Flynn. We're watching you."

The voice, the accent—Flynn recognized none of it.

"Who is this?"

The line went dead. He hoped it was a silly prank.

Flynn looked around to see if he noticed anyone suspicious. Suddenly, the entire airport appeared suspicious to him. He collected all his personal items and hurried toward ground transportation. He wanted to get out of there—and fast.

CHAPTER 16

IVAN ENJOYED SPOOKING FLYNN. It wasn't a game by any means, but the monotony of always being ahead of the people he sought to destroy, ruin, or embarrass grew old. Besides, he wasn't just having fun. He really did have eyes on Flynn. From the moment his plane landed, Ivan began receiving updates with pictures every few minutes, detailing all his movements. Yet for the moment it was pure sport, anything to distract his mind from being tucked tightly into a corner of the rafters in the U.N. general assembly hall.

His phone buzzed again.

"How are our plans coming along?" asked the voice on the other end.

"Splendidly. You have nothing to worry about," Ivan answered.

"Good. Let's keep in that way. I'll expect to hear from you tomorrow after you complete your task."

"Don't worry. It will be a good report."

"Just in case you run into trouble, I wanted to let you know I've dispatched a team to give you some added leverage."

"Excellent. And what might this leverage be?"

"I'll send you a picture."

The man hung up as Ivan awaited the image to appear on his phone. Still careful to be quiet and discreet, Ivan chuckled to himself.

"*Ideal'nyy.*" *Perfect.*

Everything was falling into place.

CHAPTER 17

WHEN FLYNN FINALLY CHECKED into the Wyndham Midtown 45 hotel just a couple blocks away from the U.N., he wondered if another coherent sentence would come out of his mouth the rest of the evening. In less than four days, he had gone from checking out a lead in Washington related to the JFK assassination to seeing footage of the elusive second gunman to receiving threats from an underground Russian extremist group he'd never heard of. It was moving too fast. He needed to stop and think. He needed a drink.

Meandering down to the hotel bar, Flynn hoped he could find a quiet table where he could mull the recent events. But there wasn't one available. And at the bar, there was just one lone seat. He reluctantly sat down and ordered a beer. If he had one request, it was to be left alone.

The portly gentleman seated to his left dashed that dream when he recognized Flynn almost immediately.

"Hey! I know you! You're James Flynn, aren't you? That conspiracy theory guy on television," he announced. The whole bar heard him.

As much as Flynn wanted to lie, he promised that he would never deny his identity to people in the public. They were lied to enough already.

"Busted. In the flesh," Flynn responded, mustering up as much personality as possible.

"Yeah, I saw you last night talking about that lady who wrote a memoir claiming she was a spy in Germany while cleaning houses. I bet she wishes she made up another fake biography now."

Flynn winced, remembering that he desecrated the woman's vulnerability. It was for her own good, but he still regretted the fact that people like the large gentleman on his left would call her a liar for the rest of her life.

The man continued to babble on about something, but Flynn tuned him out, straining to hear the latest news report on the situation brewing in Russia over the missile sites being erected. Suddenly, Flynn realized what was happening. The picture became clear in light of all the recent events. He needed to call Osborne.

Flynn threw a ten spot on the bar and left his glass of beer half full. He remembered hearing his fellow patron protest and offer to buy him another round if he stayed for a few minutes. But Flynn ignored him. *This is big. Osborne is going to thank me for this.*

"Are you sitting down?" Flynn asked Osborne the moment he picked up.

"Flynn, what are you doing calling me at home?" Osborne responded, ignoring the question.

"I figured it out. I know what's going on."

Osborne decided to ignore the fact that Flynn contacted him at his personal residence. It was a breach of protocol at the very least.

"OK, I'll humor you. What did you figure out?"

"Who was behind JFK's assassination, why I'm being followed and why I think something big is going down tomorrow at the U.N."

"Whoa, there, Flynn. Slow down. I know you're good but you're not *that* good."

"Just hear me out—It's got to be the Kuklovod. They're behind it all."

"Didn't I tell you to drop doing whatever you were investigating so they'd leave you alone?"

"You did, right. But it's too late now."

"No, it's not. Just stop chasing this story like a fool. You're going to get yourself killed."

"If I reveal that they were the shadow organization that first initiated the assassination attempt against JFK, they'll be exposed."

"And how is saying their name out loud on national television going to stop them?"

"It won't—but it will get every law enforcement agency looking for their operatives tomorrow."

"Flynn, you don't understand how these guys operate."

"Maybe not, but I don't think you do either."

"What very limited information I have on them that I can share with you is that it's a small group of individuals who like to influence world events for their own agenda. They are hardline communists."

"Exactly. Your description of them fits my theory, which is why I've been doing a lot of thinking about why they would've wanted to kill JFK."

"Please, dazzle me with your theory."

"OK, quick history lesson. Think back to 1963. Tensions between the U.S. and Russia ran high. Russia was threatening to bring missiles to Cuba to help defend them against the U.S. JFK ordered a mission into Cuba to overthrow Castro that was severely botched. It told us one thing: JFK didn't have the guts to launch a full-scale war. Those theories that the CIA wanted JFK dead because Lyndon Johnson was more likely to take U.S. troops into the Vietnam conflict—it makes sense."

"I'm following you so far. What are you getting at?"

"There's more. What happened after JFK was assassinated? Russian President Nikita Khruschev became erratic about how he wanted to handle defense. Some times he wanted to take a hard-line approach; other times he preferred diplomacy. But when he came out in the summer of 1964 and said he wanted to talk about reaching an arms treaty with the U.S., Khruschev's own political party shuttled him out faster than he could say, 'nuclear bomb.'"

"I'm still waiting for your point."

"I think the Kuklovod was trying to start a war back then—and they might be trying to do the same thing today ... in the exact same way. Except this time, they have a president who has no qualms about launching a missile in our direction."

Osborne remained quiet.

"So, what do you think?"

"Well, it's a good theory. Not sure how much of it you can prove."

"I don't care about proving it at this point. All I want to do is set every law enforcement agency on high alert for tomorrow's speech at the U.N. The last thing I want to write about is another assassination attempt. I want to write about the one nobody's ever been able to figure out—until now."

"I think you've got some good points, points that would be taken seriously if you were still an operative. But I just don't see how going on television is going to create more intense security measures tomorrow."

"Trust me, it will. Besides, the American public deserves to know that there's a group trying to infiltrate this country and wreak havoc."

"Why do they deserve to know? The public barely knows a shred of the truth when it comes to what's really going on in this country anyway."

"They deserve to know because this group killed our President and now they're trying to make a move again."

"Letting the American people stay in the dark about JFK isn't the worst thing that could happen to them."

"Yeah, but it is if this group somehow gets a foot hold again. Do you even know what *Kuklovod* means?"

Of course, Osborne knew. He didn't waste his Russian degree from Princeton.

"Yes. It means *puppeteer*," Osborne said.

"Exactly. And they're pulling the strings again. This has got to stop."

"No, what has to stop is you. I'm only going to say this one more time, so listen closely: you don't know what this organization is capable of doing. For your own sake, just let it go."

"Just hear me out, Osborne. If the Kuklovod is active again, who knows what their end game is. But all signs are pointing toward a repeat of history."

"Fine, post all your cockamamie theories on *The National*'s blog site. Just please tell me you're not going to get on television with these accusations. I'm begging you."

Flynn decided to side step the question. "Now how could I do that so quickly?"

***

IT WAS ONLY SEVEN O'CLOCK, which gave Flynn less than two hours to convince one of the cable news network programs being broadcast in New York City that he had discovered who was behind the JFK assassination. If he were anyone else, it would be an impossible task. But his name was James Flynn.

He placed a call and within minutes he was heading down to one of the area studios to share his theory with the world—a theory with proof.

It was a risky proposition at best, blurting out who killed JFK without all the hard concrete evidence necessary to publish an article. But there wasn't time. If the Kuklovod was active on American soil again, Flynn needed to do what he could to get law enforcement looking for them, if not for anything else but to heighten security tomorrow. By ten o'clock that evening, this revelation would dominate the front page of every newspaper and website in the U.S. and beyond.

Flynn knew just enough to make a splash. He had only disjointed theories as to what the Kuklovod's end game was and why they might be suddenly active in the U.S. again. What he did know was that they paid George de Mohrenschildt to orchestrate the assassination of JFK and that one of their operatives fired a bullet from a street culvert that was ultimately responsible for JFK's death. The CIA was involved in some capacity, but Flynn suspected de Mohrenschildt trusted the agency to cover his tracks. If the government that's supposed to be investigating a crime assigned the top suspect to commit that crime, their "findings" will lead nowhere. Flynn thought de Mohrenschildt was betting on it— and he bet right.

During the cab ride to the studio, Flynn called his editor and told her what he was doing. She wasn't thrilled about the idea, but she consented as long as he typed up a story with supporting media before the show aired. Flynn hung up and began pounding away on his laptop. It was a blog and most of the people were dead. If he played a little loose with the facts, he reasoned that it was OK for now. He wanted to gin up the idea that the Kuklovod was active on U.S. soil so other defense agencies would begin an aggressive search for the terrorist group's operatives. It was the best plan he could come up with on such short notice.

He even called Osborne back and gave him a courtesy heads up.

Flynn rejected Osborne's sharp protests, urging his friend and agent to call his superior and alert him to the possibility that the Kuklovod was planning an attack of some sort. It wasn't exactly the best way to secure the trust of a longtime friend, but Flynn trusted his gut more than anything—as well as Osborne's capacity to forgive him later.

CHAPTER 18

THE BRIGHT LIGHTS of the USN studio didn't bother Flynn. He thrived in this environment, especially during prime time. But moments before the show began, Flynn felt like he might throw up. This wasn't just another interview where he debunked an alien crash site in an Iowa cornfield or dismissed the idea that NASA staged the lunar landing. No, this was different. This was the moment upon which his career as a journalist would turn, where he would either achieve great credibility or be labeled a fraud.

Frances Clarke hosted USN's nine o'clock program *On the Hill*, which covered political issues of all stripes. Flynn had appeared on the program several times in the past and curried plenty of favor with Clarke. It's the only reason he was sitting in the studio on such a short notice.

Once the show began with the ominous intro music, Clarke made sure her viewers understood that tonight's show was non-nonsense and would be historic in nature. Her thick blonde hair and perky personality often gave her an edge with her interview subjects. Bedazzled by her good looks, many politicians failed to take her seriously. But when Clarke peppered her interview subjects with difficult questions, they realized they were dealing with a woman who had no qualms about eviscerating them in a matter of moments. Clips of her contentious interviews often worked their way into the 24-hour news cycle moments after the show ended. Flynn hoped she would put away the attack dog style for tonight's interview.

After ten minutes of briefly recapping the day's top political news, Clarke introduced Flynn.

"So, Mr. Flynn, you are here tonight because you want to answer a question that has haunted history buffs, politicians, and conspiracy theorists for half a century: Who was behind the JFK assassination? Was it Lyndon Johnson? Was it the CIA? Did the mob order a hit on the President? Was Clay Shaw involved? Did Russia have a hand in his death? Or perhaps Cuba? I could go on with all these theories, but why don't you tell us which of these groups is responsible for JFK's death."

Flynn paused, hoping he could deliver his pre-planned line the right way.

"Well, Frances, the answer is simple: they all did."

Clarke forced a nervous laugh, wondering if she had been taken by Flynn for a cheap publicity stunt. Her fake smile wouldn't stay plastered there for long if Flynn didn't give her what she really wanted.

"What I mean is that everyone wanted JFK dead for various reasons. But nobody did anything about it until the Kuklovod hired a CIA asset to orchestrate a plan that included Lee Harvey Oswald serving as the patsy."

Clarke furrowed her brow.

"Now, back up here for a minute. Who exactly is the Kuklovod and why have we never heard of them?"

"The Kuklovod is an extremist group dedicated to the principles of communism. And you've likely never heard of them because the CIA barely knew of their existence in the early 1960s. By the time they had plenty of information on them, the horse was out of the barn, so to speak, when it came to trying to figure out who killed JFK. And quite frankly, accusing another group would look bad since they had claimed to have their man already."

"So, why now? Why come out with this information today?"

"Because I've learned the Kuklovod is active again on U.S. soil and that they're plotting some act of terrorism very soon."

"How soon? Or can you say?"

"I can say, Frances. I believe they're going to make another attempt on the life of a U.S. President—and they're going to do it tomorrow at the U.N."

Clarke ate it up. Seconds after the words spilled out of Flynn's mouth, a ticker at the bottom of the screen captured a condensed version of the quote: "Journalist believes President's life in danger at U.N. speech."

For the rest of the interview, Clarke looked intrigued and excited, like she had struck the TV talk show lottery. And she had. Flynn picked her show to reveal one of the greatest mysteries in American politics, even if the details were sketchy and didn't make complete sense yet.

Flynn, ever the showman, refused to divulge all the details, encouraging viewers to go to *The National*'s blog if they wanted to know more and view supporting media and documents. Teasing people's curiosity on such a subject equated to mental torture. The second Flynn left the set, he imagined everyone bolting for their computers, tablets or smart phones, visiting the magazine's blog for more information.

On his way back to the Wyndham, his cell phone buzzed nearly the entire time, from text messages or voicemails. Requests for more information, and invitations to appear on other TV and radio programs streamed in. The only incoming call he answered came from his editor, Theresa.

"That was quite a show you put on tonight," Theresa said.

"Thanks. I hope what I said is taken seriously," Flynn replied.

"Well, if our web traffic is any indication, people are definitely interested. The site has already gone down twice in the past ten minutes. It's easily going to set a record for our most-read story if we can keep the site live."

"Fantastic. I hope I'm wrong about tomorrow, but I'll be here to prove myself a fool or prove myself right if they arrest someone. Either way, it's going to be a big day."

"Well, thanks for all your hard work. I knew sending you to New York was the right call."

Flynn rolled his eyes. The only reason she asked him to do it was because two other reporters were sick. Otherwise, none of this would be happening.

He decided to take the humble route.

"I appreciate the opportunity. I hope I can make you proud tomorrow, too."

Theresa wished him a good night before hanging up. Flynn couldn't help but feel like that interview would be the turning point of his career, one that was already going well. If he could make all the evidence make sense, book deals would come flying in, and so would the speaking engagements. It might give him the time and resources necessary to chase a few other conspiracy theories that befuddled him more than JFK's assassination. *Maybe I could hire an assistant, too.* He already had in mind a certain young lady from Washington.

He thought about calling her and seeing if she happened to watch his revelation of JFK's assassination conspirators. But she always went to bed around nine o'clock. Calling her at this hour wouldn't be thoughtful and might even come across as braggadocio. He could wait until the morning.

***

IVAN SAT STILL IN THE DARKNESS. His back ached even more as he remained perfectly positioned out of view. If he survived the morning security sweep, nothing would stop him from accomplishing his mission. Less than 24 hours and it would be over with.

His phone vibrated in his pocket.

"Yes," he answered.

"We've got a problem."

"I'm sure we can handle it. What is it?"

"We're going to need to get that leverage on Flynn after all. He just went on national television and said that the Kuklovod was going to kill the President tomorrow."

"Well, he's right. We are. And he won't say another word about it."

"Just handle it."

Ivan ended the call and then began texting another operative. It was a simple message:

"Get the girl."

CHAPTER 19

TODD OSBORNE ARRIVED at his office in Langley, Virginia, earlier than usual. He needed to check on the results of the photo the Vice President had sent him of Sydney. Deep down, he hoped it was real. While he never was involved romantically with Sydney, Osborne often considered asking her out. They were playful in their flirting, but neither one of them made a move. He hadn't even kissed her, though he'd wanted to on several occasions. When he found out she died, Osborne entered a depressed state for a couple of months. Hearing the news of a loved one dying is always difficult to take—but the toll of losing someone with whom you had unfinished business can create a chasm of regret in the heart. Osborne felt himself slipping into it before snapping back. He knew he might not ever find out who was behind her death, but he vowed to use every resource at his disposal if he ever had the opportunity to investigate. Yet in sixteen years, Osborne never had the chance. Seeing the image of her on his screen made him wonder if he'd lost his humanity since joining the agency.

One of the new analysts eager to curry favor with Osborne left a note on his desk. It simply read: "It's real."

Osborne sat down and sent a short note to Sandford's secret email address, alerting him to the image's authenticity. In some ways, he thought Sandford would be excited. In others, it might dredge up tortured memories best left buried. There was no telling how someone might react to the news of a loved one once believed to be dead now found alive. Osborne took the news as he might have an opportunity to tell Sydney what he always wished he had told her before she left for the Peace Corps.

A light tapping on his office doorjamb made Osborne spin around in his chair. It was Bill Barkdale. If there was one person who made Osborne's stomach turn, it was Barkdale. When Flynn uncovered what that one rogue Marine had done, Barkdale sought to silence him, claiming that it was in the interest of national security *not* to say anything. But Flynn kept pushing back, contending that the truth kept people more responsible and honest. Barkdale refused to back down, launching a personal vendetta against Flynn. In the end, Barkdale won—and had worked his way up to Deputy Directory of the CIA.

"What are you doing in here so early, Osborne?" Barkdale asked. His tone more accusatory than inquisitive.

"I've got a lot do, sir. Just trying to catch up on some work."

"You're not trying to help Flynn, are you?"

Osborne evaded the question. "What makes you think I would do a thing like that?"

"Did you see him on television last night, banging the drum of fear? He needs to realize he's not an operative any more."

"True, but he might have a point."

"That nut job wouldn't know a point if it poked him in the eye. He's just trying to sell magazines and get hits on his website. Besides, have you heard any chatter that anyone—much less the Kuklovod—is planning an attack on the President?"

Osborne decided that sharing Flynn's photo with Barkdale wouldn't be the smartest move given his aggressive tone.

"No, we haven't heard anything."

"That proves my point—Flynn is just an attention whore. He doesn't care about what's best for this country anymore. It's quite obvious to me what he's concerned with—and it's not national security."

Osborne bit his tongue. He knew Flynn was a true patriot, more so than Barkdale. But if the better part of valor is discretion, Osborne was one incredibly courageous man.

"I'll keep you posted if we hear any chatter," Osborne replied.

Barkdale left Osborne's office, heading down the hall to torture some other poor soul. The man was insufferable and wore his grudge

against Flynn on his sleeve like a military decoration. It sickened Osborne—and for the moment, it put the President's life at risk.

***

SANDFORD PERUSED HIS ITINERARY for the day. It was full of
boring meetings with members of congress trying to use him to get the
President's ear. He hated being used. *Maybe I won't have to be Briggs' lapdog
much longer.*

He also looked at the President's schedule. The two o'clock speech
to the U.N.'s general assembly was his only public appearance of the
day. Sandford suspected if anything was going to happen to the President, it was going to be then.

Suddenly, his phone buzzed, alerting him to the arrival of a new
text message:

How does President Sandford sound?

Sandford immediately deleted the message. He stared out the window and smiled. "President Sandford" sounded great. Maybe he could
actually get something done in this godforsaken town. If nobody else
there had the guts to do what was best for the country, he did. No constituents to pay back, no donors' backs to scratch. He could govern the
way a president should govern—willfully and confidently. Sandford was
going to restore faith in the republic both at home and abroad. And
Russia was going to fear the U.S.

With his thoughts drifting toward Russia, he remembered that he needed
to check his secret email account. He was anxiously awaiting Osborne's
verification as to the authenticity of the photo he received of Syndey.

Sandford didn't even need to open the message. The subject line
read: It's real.

Now Sandford hoped more than ever that he would be the President by the end of the day. He paused for a moment. The thought of
losing his friend, Arthur Briggs, was not a happy one. Despite their political differences, Sandford still considered the President his friend. But
sometimes love for country trumps friendships. For Sandford, this was
one of those times.

All he could do was sit and wait—and hope.

CHAPTER 20

FLYNN SPENT THE BETTER PART of Friday morning returning emails and phone calls regarding his bombshell interview from the night before. The news outlets had scoured all the juicy details from his blog post and were hashing and rehashing the details. Critics decried Flynn as an attention seeker, who was "devoid of depth" in his reporting. Others skewered the FBI for failing to reveal what a normal journalist could find. However, Flynn also had his fans, people who upheld his findings as "spectacular" and "earth shattering." He noticed that his subscribers to his monthly newsletter highlighting the latest conspiracy had grown by 20,000 over night. Though putting together the pieces to uncover the truth was reward enough, Flynn didn't mind reading his fan mail either.

Take that CIA. See if you can keep the American people in the dark with me around. If only I could see Barkdale's face this morning.

Flynn muttered more zingers under his breath, directed at all his detractors. It was one thing to uncover a conspiracy—one that haunted American politics for over fifty years. But more than uncovering conspiracies, Flynn loved to be right, especially when everyone was trying to prove him wrong. Yet deep down, he hoped he was wrong about the threat on the President's life. Despite his best efforts, Flynn couldn't shake it.

Natalie!

In the tidal waves of messages, he hadn't seen anything from Natalie. Surely she had heard about the newscast or seen his blog by now. Flynn imagined it had to be the topic of discussion around the water cooler at the National Archives this morning. Everyone he ever met there while researching the JFK Assassination papers freely shared their theories with him. And they were as varied as a field of snowflakes. It was almost as if each person felt the need to take widely known theories and add his or her own little twist to it. Unfortunately, Flynn ruined that fun sport by uncovering the truth, though he suspected there would still be legions of doubters who imagined the conspirators differently.

Flynn dialed Natalie's number, hoping to hear from her. Straight to voice mail. He then texted her. Five minutes passed. Nothing. *Maybe she's in a meeting.* Flynn didn't want to create doomsday scenarios in his head just yet, but he started to feel uneasy about her lack of communication—if not for her safety, for the future of their newly kindled relationship.

By lunchtime, Flynn still hadn't heard from her. He told himself that Natalie was probably busy and she'd call or text him later. Instead of worrying about it, he needed to focus his energy on preparing to cover the President's speech in a couple of hours.

***

AS FLYNN MADE HIS WAY down the street toward the U.N. building, his phone buzzed again. It was Osborne.

"So were you able to convince anyone at the agency that the President's life is in danger today?" Flynn said, skipping the formalities.

"No, but I'm convinced something is up."

"How come?"

"Listen, nobody knows about this, but I just got a call from the Vice President. He wanted me to authenticate a proof of life picture of Sydney."

Flynn didn't know he could be stunned by such news and remained silent.

"Flynn? You still there?"

"Yeah, I'm here. I ... I just can't believe that. I thought she died when those rebels attacked the school she was teaching at."

"We all did. But this photo is real," Osborne paused for a moment before continuing. "And she looks as good as ever."

"So what do you think this all means?"

"I'm not sure, but I wouldn't be surprised if something *was* up today."

"You mean, you think I'm right?"

"Unfortunately, yes."

"Did you tell Barksdale about this?"

"I told him this morning that I thought you were right and we needed to do take the potential threat seriously. He rolled his eyes and blasted you, as usual."

"That jerk."

"Yeah, but as much as he hated to admit that you might be right, he at least ordered an extra security sweep this morning."

"So, what do you want me to do? Anything?"

"I don't know. If you were going to kill the President in front of the U.N. general assembly, how would you do it?"

"I'd lie in wait. That place is like a fortress. Nobody is sneaking weapons into that place today."

"Where would you hide?"

"Where no one could find me."

"Good answer, genius. Got any ideas exactly where that location might be?"

"Not off the top of my head. But once I get there, I'll scout it out."

"The Secret Service will be there today in force, so be discreet. You know how they hate getting shown up by civilians."

"You still think of me as a civilian?"

"Of course not, but they will. Just be careful."

"I will—you know me."

"Exactly. I know you—so be careful."

Flynn tried to pretend like Osborne's words hurt, but they didn't. Osborne served as Flynn's handler long enough to know that if there was trouble to be made, Flynn would make it.

Flynn slipped his phone into his pocket and joined the crush of people trying to get through the tight security checkpoints leading into the U.N.'s general assembly hall. He wondered if he could still stop an assassin—and if he could tie the Kuklovod to JFK's assassination plot, capture them in the same day, and save the President's life, then his assignment at today's event just became far more interesting.

CHAPTER 21

PERHAPS THE MERE SUGGESTION that the President might get shot motivated the press corps to attend the Friday afternoon speech more than usual. Though Flynn didn't regularly attend U.N. speeches, he couldn't imagine this was the regular crush of reporters. Bodies jammed tightly together, shoving and pushing toward the closest entrance near press seating. Most would never see the inside of the general assembly hall, instead relegated to overflow rooms. For the lucky ones who grabbed seating inside, they sat a long distance from the podium. The U.N. placed diplomacy far above accommodating the media.

Despite his assignment to cover the speech, Flynn considered his unofficial assignment more important. He squirmed through the crush of reporters vying for the few seats in a high stakes game of musical chairs. Where he decided to watch the speech from required no seating.

Flynn walked into the room for a moment to scout it out. The U.N.'s general assembly hall was cavernous if anything. What it lacked in character it made up for with volume and innovative technology. The fact that 1,800 people could sit in this room and listen to a speech—and each person hear it in their native tongue—was remarkable if anything. Dozens of translator booths lined the back wall of the room. It was also heavily guarded and easily swept. Flynn doubted the Kuklovod had the ability to infiltrate such a guarded area that allowed only heavily vetted and credentialed translators.

The only other place that seemed more easily penetrable was the domed ceiling. Though Flynn suspected it had been swept, his CIA training taught him that hiding in such a place wasn't impossible. If the Kuklovod contained the world's best covert operatives, Flynn recognized the dome as being a possible location for a shooter—if that's how they intended to kill President Briggs.

Now Flynn only had one problem: getting past security.

He scurried around the outside of the room, looking for access to the top. Security looked tight and he needed some luck if he was going to get by. And he had to do it fast. The speech was scheduled to begin in fifteen minutes.

To get to the catwalk area inside the dome, Flynn needed to get to the roof. No other location seemed more daunting as it was always heavily guarded. On his way he needed to think of something fast.

Away from the main entrance to the room, security was more lax if not non-existent. Flynn eyed a service stairwell entrance accessed only with a security card. With a drinking fountain nearby, he began gulping down water. Flynn kept an eye fixed on the door located just ten feet away, ready to grab it once a staff worker opened it. He didn't have to wait long before someone opened the door. The heavy door nearly flung shut before Flynn could grab it, but he slipped his fingers in just in time. Before opening it all the way, he looked around to see if anyone noticed him. Everyone was too busy, lost in the minutiae of the day, to even notice him. That was the easy part.

Flynn waited until the person who opened the door disappeared through a door leading to the third floor, the highest floor adjacent to the main assembly hall. He causally walked up the steps while listening for the door. Once he passed the third floor, only two doors remained— one to the catwalk and one to the roof. He was all in now.

As Flynn continued to climb, he noticed a member of the Secret Service guarding the door to the catwalk. *This isn't going to be easy.* He climbed quietly, looking up, until the agent heard his footsteps about one flight away from the landing.

"Hey, you can't be up here!" the agent said.

"Relax, I'm CIA. Just came up here to check out what you're doing," Flynn said.

Once his face came into full view, the agent immediately recognized him.

"I know who you are and you're not CIA!"

Before the agent could alert the rest of the team what was happening, Cal struck the man's throat before landing a left and right haymaker along each of his temples. He crumpled to the ground and tumbled down several steps before coming to a stop.

"Well, I used to be CIA," Flynn said as he lifted the agent's gun and walked back up the stairs. The agent was out cold.

Flynn checked the clip of the Sig Sauer P229 .357 handgun. The last thing he wanted was to get in a gunfight atop the general assembly hall, though it would make for great theater. He simply wanted to stop the Kuklovod—if he was right. And since he had just neutralized a Secret Service agent, Flynn was betting his career that he was right.

He quietly pulled open the door leading to the catwalk. *Here we go.*

CHAPTER 22

SANDFORD WATCHED CNN's live coverage of President Briggs' speech from the U.N. He felt somewhat guilty for not caring about the content. *A famine in Central Africa? Really? We've got Russia constructing missile silos along its eastern coast—just miles away from Alaska—and we're worried about starving Africans. Gimme a break.* Sandford took the President's compassion as weakness.

President Briggs wore a tailored black suit with a non-descript blue tie. He clearly wanted the focus of his speech to be on the content, not on his appearance. It was a welcome change to the previous President who treated his position in the White House as if it were more about celebrity than statesmanship. Nevertheless, Sandford thought President Briggs had lost his way. Small points became large points of emphasis for his administration, yet he ignored the looming threat from Russia.

There was a time when African famines mattered to Sandford, too. His compassion ran deep for those in need. When he first sought to run for office, such issues drove him. He wanted to be the kind of statesman who leveraged American money and power into a force of global goodwill. It's something he learned from his compassionate-hearted daughter.

When Sydney was six years old, she heard about an orphanage in India that would be shuttered if enough generous donations didn't pour in. More than $40,000 was needed to keep the orphanage from sending its children back to the impoverished streets all alone. Sydney begged her father to build a lemonade stand so she could help. She raised $37 one Saturday and had her father mail off every penny to the orphanage. So moved by his daughter's compassion, he added $1,000 of his own money. Along with a few other generous donors she had inspired to give as well, it was all just enough to keep the orphanage open. That was the kind of effect Sydney had on people, especially Sandford. Yet he realized that she was likely going to die in captivity—where she had been for the past sixteen years—if he couldn't figure out a way to bring her home.

Lost in reminiscing about the past, Sandford's ringing cell phone whisked him back to the present.

"Ready to become President?" the voice on the other end asked after he picked up.

"Who is this?" he demanded.

The caller ignored his question. "When you take office, the first thing you need to do is authorize a new missile defense system and show Russia you mean business. If you do this, I'll know where your allegiances lie—then you must meet our other demands."

"Hey, wait —"

The line went dead.

Sandford was left alone to ponder what the call could have meant. At first he thought it was the Russian government wanting to force his hand with some type of treaty. But now he realized whoever was behind his daughter's kidnapping and staged death had a far more different agenda, an agenda that included a little sabre rattling from the U.S. It was an agenda that Sandford openly braced without any qualms.

He turned his attention back to President Briggs' speech. It was still droll and monotonous, not to mention self-serving. Sandford recognized there were far more important issues than this to tackle tonight. He could only sit and hope that maybe the events in the next few minutes might put him in a position to address them.

CHAPTER 23

FLYNN PULLED THE DOOR OPEN to the catwalk and realized handling the situation with any degree of stealth wouldn't be easy. The recessed lights circling the dome would create shadows on the floor below—and they blinded him above. The catwalk shook as he stepped onto it. He gently shut the door behind him and began walking around the circular structure.

If Flynn had one advantage, it was that of surprise. The Kuklovod's shooter—whoever he was—likely wouldn't expect anyone to scour the catwalk just as the President's speech began. Nor would he be interested in engaging in a shootout seventy-five feet above the floor. A quiet tussle suited Flynn better. When he was a CIA operative, his shooting skills were legendary. But this wasn't a range—nor had he fired a handgun in several years.

Flynn held the gun close to his body as he crept around the catwalk, looking for any sign that someone might be hiding in the beams above. If indeed a shooter was lodged in the rafters, Flynn thought it a genius position from which to eliminate a target. Not only did the beams provide cover, but so did the shining lights, making it nearly impossible to see beyond the light itself.

Halfway around, Flynn saw nothing. He realized he might appear like most of his fans to the rest of the world. *Just another tinfoil hat loon.* Even if he was right about the Kuklovod orchestrating JFK's death—which he knew he was—it would all be forgotten unless he could prove they were trying to kill another president today. Yet he remained vigilant to his self-imposed mission.

114 | R.J. PATTERSON

Just as he made it about three-fourths of the way around, he saw something. It wasn't much, but it was enough to catch his eye. A glint off a black surface. Something was moving and it shouldn't have been. That's when he recognized the gun in the hand of the shooter, pointing at the President.

"Stop!" Flynn shouted. He wished that his voice would carry more in the cavernous facility. But no one heard him—except the shooter.

Flynn pointed his gun at the shooter who slowly raised his weapon, pulling it away from its target.

"And what are you going to do about it? Shoot me?" the shooter asked, shrouding his face from Flynn.

"If I have to, yes," Flynn answered. "If you try me, you'll wish you hadn't."

"No, I'm afraid you're the one who has underestimated me, Mr. Flynn."

The fact that the man holding a gun a few feet away knew his name unnerved Flynn.

"How do you know my name?"

"Never mind that. The real question is this: Do you think you can shoot me and not suffer any consequences? I've come too far to let a little detail like this get in the way of what I'm about to do."

Flynn continued to hold his gun on the assassin. *Who is this guy?*

"I have no idea who you are—and you have no idea what you're talking about."

"Really? I don't? I wonder if Ms. Hart would appreciate you being so cavalier with her life."

Flynn froze. He pondered for a moment if the shooter was bluffing.

"You don't know where she is. She's at her office, probably watching the President's speech."

"Oh, she's watching the speech right now, but she's not at the office. And you can bet she's rooting for me to shoot the President—it's the only way she gets to go home."

Flynn attempted to reason with the man, anything to stall and possibly get a better look at his face.

"Just throw the gun over here so I won't have to kill you. I'd have to blow your head off up here. It'd make such a difficult mess to clean up."

The shooter stopped and stared at Flynn. "You think this is all a game, don't you? Well, it's not. Like I said before, you've underestimated me if you don't think I've thought of everything."

The shooter paused for a moment before continuing.

"So just remember if you pull that trigger, you're also pulling the trigger on your little girlfriend's life as well. If my friends don't hear from me in thirty minutes, they're going to kill her. Understand?"

That voice. Where do I know it from?

Flynn couldn't discern if the shooter was bluffing or not. It wasn't a chance he wished to take.

Yet as Flynn stood there, processing what the man just said, the assassin pulled out his gun and aimed it at President Briggs. The assassin's face was in plain view.

Ivan!

"No!" Flynn yelled as he lunged toward the shooter.

It was too late. Ivan's shot was true.

President Briggs crumpled to the floor in front of a stunned assembly.

CHAPTER 24

SANDFORD GAWKED AT THE SCREEN, struggling to believe what he just witnessed. Even though he suspected it was a possibility—even though a nutty reporter went on the news the night before and said it could happen—Sandford couldn't believe it. His friend—and President of the United States, Arthur Briggs—writhed in pain on the floor in a chaotic scene in front of the entire U.N. general assembly.

Some Secret Service agents helped him up and rushed him off the main floor. Others gazed skyward, searching for where the shot came from. In an effort to escape the horrific scene, delegates dashed through the doors and lobby. An overhead camera from a local helicopter captured the surreal scene of frantic delegates spilling out into the street.

The television commentator tried to make sense of what had just happened. She stammered over her words, doing well to remember that *The National's* investigative reporter, James Flynn, had forewarned the nation about such a plot. Despite many reporters attending the speech, in case something did happen, no one was prepared for the blood sport, based on their bumbling reports. Seeing the leader of the free world gunned down made for compelling television—but it unnerved even the most composed anchors.

Sandford didn't have a chance to hear any more of the reports before he was ordered to go with Secret Service agents as a precautionary measure. Protocol demanded that in the event of an attempted assassination on the President's life, the Vice President would be taken to a safe place until further notice. Sandford didn't like the idea of being cut off from the outside world, but it was something he could endure if he was going to find his way behind the desk in the Oval Office.

The phone in his pocket buzzed. He figured it was his wife, checking in with him and see how he was doing. He was wrong. It was a text message.

How do you feel now, Mr. President?

Sandford stared at the screen for a few moments before sliding it back into his pocket. He thought he would feel happy, being the acting President, if not the permanent one. But he felt sick to his stomach. Guilt overwhelmed him, as if he had a hand in his friend's demise, possibly even his death. *I should have said something.*

A staffer shoved a piece of paper into his hand. It was a security brief regarding the missile silos being erected in Siberia. According to satellite photos, it appeared that five silos were already operational. Intelligence reports suspected another five would be operational by week's end. It was enough to help Sandford remember why he never said anything. If Russia wanted to bang the drums of war, the U.S. better disrupt the beat. *Briggs or no Briggs, the country needs me right now. And they need me more than ever.*

CHAPTER 25

IVAN GLARED DOWN AT FLYNN. He was sure his shot accomplished the job, but he didn't appreciate Flynn's brazen attempt to distract him. By the time Flynn reached him, where he was wedged between a structural beam and the wall, the bullet had long left the chamber headed for President Briggs. Ivan quickly grabbed the barrel of his rifle and used it as a battering ram against Flynn's head.

With Flynn moaning on the ground, Ivan scuttled Flynn's pistol a safe distance away from him.

"Get up," Ivan barked. "We've got to move now—unless you want me to leave you here with the weapon, after I wipe it down."

Flynn staggered to his feet, moving groggily.

"Here, put this on," Ivan said, tossing an FBI windbreaker in his direction. "Put this hat on, too. God, I love American merchandise."

Once Flynn regained his composure and put on the FBI disguise, Ivan would've sworn he was a real agent.

Ivan, still wearing his catering uniform, led them through a ventilation shaft that allowed them to slip down to the third floor. With the chaos emptying the building, nobody even noticed them merge into the crowd and make their way out to the street.

Once outside, Ivan felt Flynn resist his firm grasp as if he might try to make a dash to escape. Ivan tightened his grip and pulled Flynn's ear closer to his mouth so he could hear him.

"If you want to see your girlfriend alive again, you won't do anything stupid. Understand?"

Flynn nodded and relaxed, continuing to follow Ivan's lead through the mass hysteria.

After another hundred yards, they arrived at the curb, where a dummy news van awaited with its doors wide open. Ivan's cousin, Andrei, was driving.

"Hurry up and get in," Andrei said. "We need to get moving before they quarantine the area."

Ivan shoved Flynn to the back of the van where another operative zip tied his hands and feet.

"You're not going anywhere for a while unless you know some magic tricks," he said as he yanked on the tie to make sure Flynn had no chance at escape.

Ivan slapped the inside of the van wall twice and off they went.

He then edged next to Flynn and whispered in his ear.

"That was a stupid thing you did back there," he said. "You almost made me miss. Fortunately for you—and your girlfriend—I'm not easily rattled. You just better hope your President died from that shot. If he didn't, I'm holding you personally responsible. You might have to die in his place."

Ivan watched Flynn's hand shake.

"You nervous?" Ivan said, gesturing toward Flynn's hands.

Flynn shook his head.

"Well, you should be. My boss says if you prove to be useful, you can live. Once you start being unuseful—"

Ivan made a throat slashing motion with his thumb.

It only made Flynn tremble more.

"Don't worry. You'll get to see your girlfriend in a few minutes. Maybe she can kiss your forehead and make it feel all better."

Ivan laughed out loud before slamming his elbow against Flynn's forehead and banging him into the side of the van. The vicious hit knocked Flynn out again.

Staring at the reporter, Ivan almost felt sorry for him. *If you would've just stuck with the story I gave you, you wouldn't be in this mess.*

Ivan leaned against the van wall and reflected on the events of the previous hour. His back still ached, but his heart felt good. He had been training his whole life for something like this, hoping that he could be part of influencing change in the world. Good change.

He glanced at Flynn, who started to edge back into consciousness. Ivan bashed his head against the van wall one more time, putting him out again. *When he wakes up, he'll have no idea where he is.* He then took Flynn's phone, turned it off, and tossed it out the window.

Fifteen minutes later, they arrived at a warehouse used as a staging area for all of the Kuklovod's operations. Ivan grabbed Flynn by the back of his jacket and led him to the door. He proudly showed his catch to the three other men, who offered a light-hearted applause as they congratulated him on a successful operation.

"Is he dead yet?" Ivan asked to no one in particular.

"Who?" one of the men asked.

"The President, you idiot. Who else do you think I'm talking about?"

"Not yet, but from the sound of it, he won't be alive much longer. That was one heck of a shot, Ivan."

Ivan beamed with pride as he shoved Flynn toward one of the men.

"Lock him up with the girl," he said. "They may still be of some use to us yet."

One of the guards slammed Flynn's head against the wall, knocking him out cold again. He dragged Flynn's body across the floor before sliding him into the room with Natalie and locking the door.

Ivan then sat down in front of the small television set placed on an empty desk near one of the barren walls. It wasn't often that he got to watch his target die on national television. He grabbed a bottle of vodka out of the bottom drawer and took a long pull on it. It was almost time to celebrate.

CHAPTER 26

OSBORNE STORMED DOWN THE HALL toward the conference room. The stack of operational papers in his hand meant little to him now. *If Barksdale's ego wasn't so big, we wouldn't be in this mess right now.* He entered the room and sat down in the closest empty seat, slamming his papers down in front of him. The agents already present buzzed about how the Secret Service let such a thing happen. It only made Osborne angrier. *This was our nightmare to stop and we did nothing.*

Osborne seethed, unwilling to engage in any speculation with the others as to the whereabouts of the shooter or the chance of survival for the President. He joined the agency to serve his country, to protect the ones he loved. Yet an incident like this made Osborne question his competency, as well as that of the entire agency. He wondered how directors and agents let their egos mitigate their ability to make wise snap decisions. Perhaps he was making more of the situation than he should have, extrapolating an isolated incident with one bull-headed director across the entirety of the CIA. Nevertheless, the happenings in the past hour gnawed at him.

Instead of casting blame, Osborne realized that he needed to focus on the task at hand: locating and capturing the shooter.

When Barksdale breezed into the briefing, nobody was ready for what he was about to say.

"Quiet everybody!" Barksdale hissed.

He glared at each person around the table, spending more time looking at Osborne more than any other person. It made Osborne uneasy.

"We have our first lead—and we are working with other law enforcement branches to find who we believe is our shooter," Barksdale said, gesturing toward the screen. "This is who we think shot President Briggs."

Osborne's jaw dropped, leaving him staring at the screen in disbelief.

"You've got to be kidding me!" Osborne blurted out.

It was a picture of James Flynn.

Barksdale looked up from his papers and shot a nasty look toward Osborne.

"I wish I was, but all the evidence points to him at this point as being our shooter," Barksdale said.

"What evidence?"

"This evidence," Barksdale said, pointing to the flat screen on the wall where pictures were uploaded.

The first picture was of an agent lying unconscious—or maybe even dead—in a stairwell.

"This is Trey Madison, a Secret Service agent immobilized by James Flynn."

Barksdale scrolled to the next set of images, one of Flynn walking with another man through the crowd to a van with an open door with another one of them getting into a waiting van with an open door.

"You can't tell if he's leading that operation or if he's a hostage," Osborne said, defending Flynn.

"He'll have his chance to defend himself without you making up theories for him," Barksdale said.

Osborne looked at the papers in front of him. He felt the uneasy stare of Barksdale fall on him. Osborne looked up. Barksdale looked like he might eat Osborne on the spot.

"Do you know how James Flynn knew there was going to be an attempt on the President's life today? It's because he was going to make it! Wake up, Osborne!"

Osborne shifted nervously in his chair, uneasy with the operational plan being put in place—and even more so of Barksdale's determination to pin the assassination attempt on Flynn. The public would find delicious irony in such a story if Barksdale rushed to leak this to the press. But Osborne hated it.

He knew Flynn was innocent—now he had to prove it before he could save him.

CHAPTER 27

HOLED UP WITH A CADRE of Secret Service agents and White House staffers, Sandford wondered if this was really happening. People intended to kill the President with surprising regularity, yet the Secret Service and the FBI thwarted most attempts. And the public rarely heard about them. Sandford couldn't believe someone actually succeeded—almost.

The staffers huddled as they discussed protocol for introducing Sandford as the acting President. A pair of speechwriters began working on Sandford's speech informing the country of Briggs' death. But it was all premature.

Despite the furious preparation taking place, Briggs remained alive, fighting for his life as doctors worked to save him. The reports flowed out of the hospital and to staffers every five to ten minutes—mostly updates on what the doctors planned to do or what procedures they were utilizing. None of it meant anything to Sandford. He just wanted to know if Briggs was going to live or die. And that was a question no one dared attempt to answer at the moment.

Amid the flurry of activity, Sandford slunk into a chair lodged in the corner of the room. Without any decisions to be made, he used the time to think and reflect. In a matter of hours, he could be announced as the new President of the United States, the leader of the free world. Just a few days before when he started receiving the anonymous calls and texts, he dreamed about what such a moment would mean to him. In his mind, it was grand. *Gerald Sandford, the most powerful man in the world.*

But that's not how he felt now. Feelings of guilt and shame overtook him. *Arthur Briggs, my friend, would still be alive if I had said something.* Maybe he was right, yet there was no way of knowing for sure. If this secret group—whoever they were—wanted Briggs dead and him to be President, they likely would've found another way to make it happen.

More than anything, Sandford worried if he would be able to govern like he needed to. *Will they use Sydney's life to control me? What if I say no?* Those were real questions that demanded answers. But Sandford had no way of answering them.

Sandford tried to put things in perspective—the country needed *him*, not weak-stomached Briggs. With Russia threatening U.S. security daily, the American people needed a leader who wasn't afraid to go on the offensive and protect them from danger. Briggs would never authorize a pre-emptive strike. But Sandford? He *dreamed* of launching missiles on the country where his daughter disappeared. His thirst for revenge overwhelmed him.

Conflicted feelings aside, Sandford's major concern was figuring out how to extract his daughter from the clutches of the Russians without starting a major war. Apparently, they had her—and they had her all along. But could he find her? And could he legally authorize a tactical team to rescue her? It was his daughter. He'd get on a helicopter and go rescue her himself if he knew where she was being held. His fantasy of bravado was interrupted by a staffer making an announcement.

"I just got word from the hospital and it isn't good," he said. "President Briggs made it through surgery but then he took a turn for the worse. He's on life support now and his organs are shutting down. If you're the praying type, now would be the time to start."

Sandford wanted to pray. It was part of his daily routine in the morning. He always read his Bible and prayed. But he couldn't put his heart into it. *What kind of demented person prays for a man he wants to die?* He couldn't even muster up the words in his head, much less mean them. *What does the Bible say? God appoints government leaders? What if this is what God wants?*

Sandford concluded he couldn't be sure if divine intervention was playing a role in Briggs' death—and he wouldn't presume to know what God wanted. But Sandford wanted it, mixed feelings and all. He wanted to take charge. He wanted to save America. He wanted to save his daughter.

CHAPTER 28

WHEN FLYNN AWOKE, he moaned. It took him a few moments to realize where he was and what he was doing there. Fortunately, he didn't forget who Natalie was.

"Are you OK? What happened?" she said, scooting next to him on the floor.

Flynn appreciated her empathy. Her compassion for others was one of the traits he admired about her. Apparently, it wasn't reserved for orphaned children in Africa, refugees in Washington, or cats with broken legs in her neighborhood. Even a battered reporter could be the beneficiary of her care and concern.

Slumped against the wall, Flynn looked up at Natalie and smiled.

"You should see the other guy," he said, trying to get her to smile. It worked.

"I'm glad to see they didn't beat your sense of humor out of you," she said.

"It's about the only thing they didn't beat out of me."

She smiled then furrowed her brow. "Do you remember what happened?"

"Oh, I don't think I'll ever forget it."

"Before I tell you, let me ask you something: are *you* OK?"

While Flynn struggled to regain his wits after getting beat to hell, he realized that Natalie likely had no idea what was going on.

"I'm fine. I figured it all out," she said.

"Well, maybe you can fill me in because the last couple of hours are a little fuzzy."

"These guys wanted to kill the President. You tried to stop them— but they knew you would. So, they kidnapped me to deter you. Does that about sum it up?"

"Well, you're much sharper than I give you credit for."

Natalie ignored his comment.

"I overheard them talking about their plans—it wasn't that difficult really."

"I never realized you spoke Russian."

"I *listen* in Russian. Speaking is a different matter."

"Glad to see you haven't lost your sharp wit, either," Flynn said.

Natalie smiled again before stroking Flynn's face with the back of her hand. She looked awkward caressing his cheek with the back of her zip-tied hands, but Flynn appreciated the gesture.

"So are you going to tell me what happened out there?" she asked.

Flynn detailed the events that led up to his capture—the veiled threats against him, the television interview, how he muscled his way through security, and his showdown on the catwalk above the U.N.'s general assembly hall. He resisted the urge to embellish. The story seemed fanciful enough without him adding in unnecessary—and un-true—details just to make him look more like a real action hero. The truth worked fine, though he winced when telling her about his capture and how he let the shooter get a shot off.

Natalie shared the details of her abduction as well. She had gone to bed early that evening only to be awoken from a deep sleep by armed masked men who stormed into her room. They gagged and bound her before taking her outside to a waiting van. No one saw them as they left, her muffled screams absorbed only by the still night air.

After she finished, she asked the only question that mattered.

"So, how are we going to get out of here?"

"That's a good question. Let's see if we can find out what's going on first."

Flynn scooted across the concrete floor on his butt. He lay down and looked beneath the small crack between the floor and the bottom of the door. Natalie followed suit. Flynn counted three guards, none of whom appeared to be all that imposing to him. He strained his ears to hear what they were saying. Most of the conversation centered around the President's condition. Only one of the guards appeared to speak English, as he listened to the broadcast and translated what the commentators were saying. President Briggs' condition appeared to be worsening. And so was Flynn's fate.

"Это - позор, он никогда не будет жить, чтобы рассказать его историю," said one of the guards.

"Did you get that?" Flynn asked.

"Yeah, I got it—'It's a shame he will not live to tell his story,'" Natalie answered, confirming what Flynn thought he heard.

Flynn needed to find a way out of there—and fast.

CHAPTER 29

MINUTES TICKED PAST LIKE HOURS for Sandford as the clock struck ten on Friday evening, nearly eight hours since the assassination attempt. Updates from the hospital slowed as doctors settled in for the night to monitor the President's vitals while in a coma. None of the latest reports were hopeful as the mood became one akin to a deathwatch.

Josh Pickens, the White House Chief of Staff, walked toward Sandford. The usually spry Pickens appeared dour and looked like he had aged several years in less than a day.

"I think you need to consider looking this over," Pickens said, reluctantly handing Sandford a sheet of paper.

It was a copy of the 25th Amendment to the U.S. Constitution.

When the Constitution was first written, the language in Article I, Section 2, surrounding how the Vice President might assume office in the event that the President became incapacitated was vague at best. There needed to be a clear way to determine how the President would be declared unfit to lead—and there needed to be a designated body of people to make this happen. In 1967, the 25th Amendment was ratified, providing a clear path to the presidency in such an unlikely event. Today, the unlikely became reality.

Sandford stared at the memo, citing Section 4 of the 25th Amendment:

Whenever the Vice President and a majority of either the principal officers of the executive departments or of such other body as Congress may by law provide, transmit to the President pro tempore of the

Senate and the Speaker of the House of Representatives their written declaration that the President is unable to discharge the powers and duties of his office, the Vice President shall immediately assume the powers and duties of the office as Acting President.

This is really happening. I'm going to be President.

"Mr. Sandford, some of the cabinet members are reluctant to move on this so quickly," Pickens said. "They want to give it time to play out before they cede control of the office to you. But I don't believe we can afford to wait, given some of the situations facing our country right now."

Sandford nodded, but then questioned Pickens' motives.

"Why are you doing this, Josh? Aren't you supposed to be fighting for your boss to keep his job right now?"

"If the situation were any different, I would, Mr. Sandford." He then leaned in close to add in a whisper, "But I agree with you on foreign policy. And we need your brazen leadership right now—or I fear something far worse than we ever imagined will happen."

As Pickens pulled back, Sandford winked at him.

"I'll try not to let you down," Sandford said.

"Don't just do it for me—do it for the American people."

With that, Pickens vanished into the stream of staffers scurrying about the room.

Sandford smiled. He needed to draft a declaration. The office was almost his.

CHAPTER 30

WHILE NEARLY EVERY AGENT TURNED their focus on apprehending James Flynn, Osborne had a different agenda. If perhaps the Kuklovod were holding Flynn hostage, and if law enforcement found Flynn, then they would catch the real assassin. But Osborne knew how these things went. In a situation like this, nobody is innocent until proven guilty. The public, along with every politician and government agency wanting to claim an easy victory, will want to swing someone from the gallows first—and ask questions later. Restraint was lost in times like these.

Osborne mulled over what he knew. The President was shot, just as Flynn had predicted on television the night before. Flynn assaulted a Secret Service agent and took his gun. Flynn was caught on a security camera impersonating an FBI agent before vanishing into the crowd. Osborne admitted to himself that things looked bad for Flynn. If it couldn't get any worse, the FBI found Flynn's cell phone lying in a gutter near the U.N. All signs pointed toward a hit and escape plan—one that was premeditated if it included an FBI jacket and hat.

Without much else to go on, Osborne felt defeated. He only had one idea that could possibly turn around the investigation and point it to the right people. It could also result in a suspension or dismissal. Barksdale seemed irritable at best, and Osborne wondered if now was the time to present the only bit of evidence he had. After pondering every possible outcome, he decided to take a chance. Time was running short if every agency didn't turn their focus on hunting the real assassin.

Osborne walked down the hall toward the command room serving as the operational headquarters for this manhunt. Barksdale snipped at an analyst and shoved a paper into his chest before turning to his next victim. Though Barksdale's irritable mood made this an inopportune time, Osborne wondered if there ever was a good time to bring something to the deputy director.

"I think I have something you might want to see," Osborne said, tentatively offering a folder to Barksdale.

"If it's not a report on the capture of James Flynn, I don't want to see it," he barked.

"Sir, I think you really need to take a look."

Barksdale flipped open the folder and saw the surveillance camera footage of Ivan talking with Flynn several days before at The Liaison in Washington, D.C.

"Who is this guy with Flynn?" Barksdale asked.

"That's Ivan the Terrible. He's one of the Kuklovod's top operatives."

"Well, thank you, Mr. Osborne, for more evidence to throw at James Flynn. Conspiring with the Kuklovod, the same group he accused of being behind the JFK assassination. No wonder he knew they were going to attempt to shoot the President. He was working with them."

"He wasn't working with them. They were trying to prevent him from talking about the group publicly."

"You have a fanciful imagination, Mr. Osborne. Where did you get this picture anyway?"

"Flynn sent it to me several days ago."

"What for?"

"He thought some group was trying to keep him from finding out the truth behind the JFK assassination. He sent it to me so I could help identify the guy."

"And you gave out classified information to James Flynn?"

"I thought he might want to know who he was dealing with. And I warned him to stand down."

"A lot of good that did!"

"Look, I know —"

"I'm done with you. I need all hands on deck now, but when this search is over with, you're suspended. And if I find out you spent one more minute after this conversation trying to prove Flynn's innocence, I'm going to make sure you never sniff another government job the rest of your life. Do you understand me?"

Osborne nodded and walked away. He felt more defeated than when he began.

But it didn't take long for that to change.

Osborne heard one of the analysts shout gleefully about some footage she found. She transferred it to the main monitor so everyone could see. It was a security camera that showed Flynn being led away by a man holding a gun closely to Flynn's back.

"We need to be looking for *that* guy," the analyst said, pointing at Ivan.

Barksdale jumped in. "OK, people. It looks like we have a hostage situation here and we need to let all other law enforcement know about it. And get me an ID on that shooter."

Osborne glared at Barksdale. "I think we already know who he is."

Barksdale didn't even acknowledge Osborne's find. "Everybody, we're looking for Ivan the Terrible, a Kuklovod operative. He's trained, armed and dangerous. Get a BOLO out on him right now. Move it!"

Osborne returned to his office, feeling vindicated. Now if they could only find Flynn before Ivan put a bullet in his head.

CHAPTER 31

SATURDAY MORNING STARTED with a flurry of activity for Gerald Sandford. Becoming the President of the United States overnight isn't a smooth process, no matter what the Constitution allows. Convincing resistant cabinet members that it was in the best interest of the country to hand over power to him wasn't easy.

Sandford's staunchest opposition came at the hands of Diane Dixon, the Secretary of Education. Dixon never liked Sandford for a number of reasons. First and foremost was the fact that he unseated her late husband in a Tennessee senate race. Despite her southern charm and uncanny ability to convince people to do whatever she wanted them to, Dixon didn't fool Sandford. She possessed an ulterior motive for every action she took. Her antics annoyed Sandford so much that he even came up with his own nickname for her: Dixon the Vixen. There wasn't an ounce of love lost between the two, and Sandford wasn't surprised at her strong resistance to joining the rest of the cabinet in declaring the President unfit to lead. When questioned by Josh Perkins as to the reason for her reluctance to sign the letter, she quipped, "A comatose Briggs is better than a fully coherent Sandford any day."

Nevertheless, she eventually joined the others and signed the letter, requesting that power be transferred to Sandford immediately.

By noon, the power of transfer was complete. Wearing a dark suit with a red power tie, Sandford even looked the part when he assumed his new leadership role. An hour later, he addressed the nation:

"Good afternoon, fellow Americans.

"As you know, we have all struggled with the news—and graphic images—of our beloved President, Arthur Briggs, getting shot yesterday afternoon during a speech at the U.N. The President and I have been friends for years, and seeing him shot like that pained me to no end. We will not stand for an attack against our leader, and I guarantee you we will exhaust every resource we have to track down the person or group responsible for this travesty and bring them to justice.

"Meanwhile, while President Briggs fights for his life, we still have a battle of our own to fight, one that involves a disconcerting swell of aggressive talk of war from Russia.

"As a result, the President's cabinet decided it best to maintain a presence of leadership during such difficult times. While we all hope and pray for the President's full and speedy recovery, the cabinet has invoked Section Four of the Twenty-Fifth Amendment, which allows me to serve as acting President.

"Our office will provide the media and consequently the American public with daily updates on the progress of President Briggs' recovery.

"Also as my first act as President, I want to announce a new special weapons defense program that we will begin building in earnest, immediately."

"Thank you for your time and your prayers. May God bless America."

The moment the camera turned off, Sandford removed his microphone and stepped from behind the podium, greeted by several staffers who congratulated him on a well-delivered speech.

"You looked very presidential, sir," said one staffer.

The butt kissing has already begun.

He rolled his eyes. He was more interested in doing some butt kicking—namely, the Russians'—and getting his daughter back home.

He stepped into the Oval Office, his phone buzzing with a text message:

Well done, sir. Now time to take action.

Sandford hated feeling like someone's puppet, though no one had yanked any strings yet—as long as he overlooked the assassination attempt on the President. Other than that, the text messages were annoying and sometimes informational, particularly regarding his daughter.

No one is going to tell me what to do. I'm the President of the United States.

A staffer approached Sandford with a stack of documents.

"Here you go, Mr. President. I thought you might want to see these," he said, handing Sandford the papers.

Mr. President. Now, that's what I like to hear.

He smiled and thanked the staffer for the information. He needed to sit down. There was work to be done.

He had some missiles to prepare to launch.

CHAPTER 32

FLYNN AWOKE LATE SATURDAY MORNING with an aching back and a stiff neck. It was like most mornings for him. Except now his arms and legs were zip tied together—and he lay on the floor. He squinted as he looked around the room. A small vertical window at the very top of the room provided a scant amount of light, but it was enough to see Natalie in all her morning glory. Still asleep, Natalie's hair remained matted to the side of her face, her mouth slightly open. *At least she looks cute in the morning before she gets ready for the day.* Not that Flynn really cared, but it was a nice bonus.

Those were the types of thoughts that kept Flynn going. Less than forty-eight hours ago he reveled in victory, solving one of the greatest mysteries in U.S. history: Who was behind the JFK assassination plot. But none of that mattered. He didn't want to think about his legacy, determining that he wasn't done creating it yet. Flynn wanted to tell more stories and expose more lies. He wanted to live.

But such desires seemed like nothing more than dreams at this point, locked in a cell and immobilized. While freedom would be nice, he would settle for a piece of bread and water.

He scooted back toward the door to see if there was any movement going on outside. He noticed two larger men sitting in chairs with their arms folded and heads slumped down. They both wore black tank tops with green Army surplus pants and boots. Tattoos covered the arms of both men. Flynn wanted the men to be dead, but he recognized that they were simply asleep. The third guard, who was wearing a black turtleneck shirt and similar pants to his cohorts, walked around the room with a cup of coffee in his hand, pistol holstered on his hip. Ivan was nowhere to be seen.

Flynn looked back at Natalie against the wall. She stirred but continued to sleep.

The phone belonging to the lone awake guard rang, allowing Flynn to listen in on one side of the conversation. His Russian was rusty, but he understood the gist of the conversation: The plan was running according to schedule and they would have no need of the hostages after tonight, once they moved locations.

Flynn heard Natalie stirring and began sliding back toward her.

"What is it, James? What's going on out there?" she asked.

He ignored her question. "I bet you didn't know how beautiful you look in the morning."

She smiled and rolled her eyes. "You're not answering my question."

Flynn was well aware he was evading her question.

"Has anyone ever told you that before?"

She smiled again, continuing to mildly protest. "Stop it, James."

"I'm serious. Has anyone ever told you that?"

"Gosh, you are relentless—and ridiculous. We're hostages of some terrorist group I've never heard of and you want to pay me compliments."

"Well, have they?"

She laughed again and shook her head.

"Now that you know I've never been told that before, will you please answer my question? What are they saying out there?"

Flynn paused, choosing his words carefully.

"I'd really rather not say."

"Come on, James," said Natalie, her patience wearing thin. "What are they saying?"

"OK, fine. I'll tell you. They said that after tonight they don't have need for us any more and they will need to get rid of us."

"Get rid of us? I'm hoping that means let us go."

"Nice try. But you know that's not what they mean."

"What are we gonna do?"

Flynn shrugged his shoulders. "I'm working on it."

Ever since he'd been tossed into this room with Natalie, he'd been "working on it." But nothing was working in his head, at least not a plan that guaranteed safety for both of them. As much as he wished he had hours to plan out an escape, time was a precious commodity—and it was vanishing quickly.

He knew how high the stakes were. It was time to figure a way out of there.

CHAPTER 33

TODD OSBORNE STUDIED THE MESSAGE on his computer, wondering if all of the events over the past week were some orchestrated move by the Kuklovod. For an extremist terrorist group, their movements were so infrequent that the CIA often considered declaring them defunct. And then something would happen. A bombing here. A kidnapping there. A sudden rise to power by an unknown politician who was sympathetic to Kuklovod type causes. It was just enough to show a pulse, that the organization still had operatives—and still had an agenda.

But this week's events meant something bigger was up. The Kuklovod remained covert except when it was preparing to make a big move on the global scene. And if ever there seemed like a big move, Osborne concluded this was it. Everything seemed to be falling into place. The removal of a peace-loving President. The re-emergence of the Vice President's supposedly dead daughter. The distraction of a former CIA operative who chose to finger the organization on national television as a group targeting the President.

The message on Osborne's terminal was from an operative embedded in Russia. He taught English at a school in the Urals and rarely had much contact of any kind. If Siberia was where Russia sent political opponents to silence them, the Urals was where the CIA sent operatives who barely passed key components of the agency's espionage training. Nothing ever happened there, at least, nothing to speak of. But Osborne wondered if one of his operatives had discovered one of the most elusive locations in global spydom: the location of the Kuklovod's headquarters.

Most agents figured out quickly why they were there. If they avoided detection, they would usually be reassigned within a couple of years. Normally, Osborne would've dismissed this as an overzealous agent, trying to make a name for himself. But with the sudden re-emergence of the Kuklovod injecting themselves into national events, he couldn't dismiss this as mere coincidence. Something far sinister seemed at play.

Identified two Kuklovod operatives. Followed them to what appears to be Kuklovod HQ. Please advise.

Osborne wanted to storm the gates and oust the terrorists in a public display—something the agency would frown upon, especially since the U.S. wasn't officially in Russia. And this opportunity seemed worth breaking protocol. But not when tensions with Russia were so high—and not when he was unsure of the Kuklovod's end game. He advised the operative to continue monitoring the situation. Osborne wanted to discover more before charging in—much more.

CHAPTER 34

BREAKING FREE OF THE ZIP TIE holding Flynn's hands behind his back never presented a serious problem. However, severing the tie without an action plan would prove detrimental to his hopes of escaping if he didn't have a firm plan in place. From experience, Flynn knew plans executed with confidence worked. Trying to escape without a plan? Not the best idea—especially when you had someone with you.

"So what are we going to do?" Natalie asked.

"Escape," Flynn responded dryly.

"Well, I hope so. But how?"

"I'm working on it."

Flynn slid next to the door and put his ear to the ground to discern what their captors were saying. A few moments passed in silence as Flynn strained to listen.

"Well?" Natalie asked, finally breaking the silence.

"Well, what?"

"Well, what did you hear?"

"Nothing that's going to help us right now."

"What were they saying?"

"Do you really want to know?"

"Of course I do. If I'm a spy now, I want to know what's going on."

Flynn cracked a slight smile. "OK then, I'll tell you. They said they hope that everything goes as planned in the missile attack on the United States—and that they are a long ways away when it happens."

Natalie had no idea how to process such information. She remained quiet, staring at the floor.

"I told you that you didn't want to know," Flynn said, attempting to break Natalie out of her stupor. "So, even if we make it out of here alive, we're going to get bombed. What do you think about that?"

Natalie stayed quiet, rocking slowly and staring at the floor.

"OK, I see that you are having a hard time with this. Well, you need to snap out of it because we're about to break out of here."

Natalie's gaze broke and she rejoined Flynn in the present. "What do you want me to do?"

Sharing his detailed plan with Natalie, Flynn expressed full confidence that his idea would result in freedom.

Flynn sliced his zip tie and climbed up the wall and into the beams of the room's vaulted ceiling.

"Ready?" he asked Natalie.

She nodded. Flynn could tell she wanted to believe in his plan but looked tentative at best.

"Sell it hard," Flynn said.

She nodded again and smiled slightly.

A moment later, Natalie unleashed a scream that pierced the ears of the three guards. One of them came rushing into the room.

"What is wrong?" he asked, seeing Natalie lying on the floor.

Before the guard received an answer, Flynn jumped down from the rafters and onto the guard's back. In one fell swoop, he broke the guard's neck and watched the man slump to the floor. He then scurried back up into the room's rafters.

One of the remaining guards called out and waited. Receiving no reply from his comrade, he rushed into the room.

Natalie screamed again as she shifted her glare toward the guard lying on the floor next to her. Again Flynn descended, breaking the man's neck. However, he struggled enough to alert the other guard that something wasn't right.

When the lone remaining guard charged into the room, Flynn was ready. He had lifted two guns off the dead guards and readied himself.

The final guard never saw his two fallen comrades before succumbing to his own death in a hail of bullets. Flynn hated dragging out confrontations, especially when they were easy to end. He glanced at Natalie, who looked like she might throw up.

"Being a spy isn't easy," he said. "This is the part of the job that's hard to take."

Sullen, Natalie sat on the floor, staring at the sudden body count that resulted from Flynn's plan.

"It'll be all right," he said. "They got what was coming to them."

"What if they could've helped you and given you more information about what they were up to?" she asked.

"They already did."

He offered Natalie his hand to help her up. She reached for it and was instantly pulled to her feet.

There was still no sign of Ivan.

Flynn spent the next fifteen minutes taking pictures and videos of the building from one of the dead guard's phones. It would be valuable for law enforcement to determine the organization's next move—assuming Flynn didn't figure it out first.

CHAPTER 36

SANDFORD WALKED INTO THE CABINET MEETING and closed the doors behind him. He had been in debates that were less contentious than the one going on in the room he now presided over. Despite his best efforts to ignore the buzz of staffers in the hall, Sandford understood the situation, ruled by chaos and confusion. Some staffers quietly whispered how Sandford could take over the White House like he did. Others wondered aloud who was behind the assassination attempt, questioning if it was an inside job. All the while, television and radio reports being monitored depicted nothing short of anarchy outside the Capitol steps. Protesters had already taken to the streets, demanding the U.S. strike whoever did this to their Commander-in-Chief. While no group had claimed responsibility, based on the signs toted by angry citizens, the instigators ranged from Middle Eastern terrorist organizations to Syria, Iran, China and Russia. It was clear nobody understood the situation at hand. And neither did Sandford.

He poured himself a glass of water before assuming the chair previously occupied by President Briggs. Sinking into the leather chair, Sandford felt good. Whatever was going on was his problem now—and he was going to fix it. But he first needed to create solidarity with Briggs' cabinet members.

"I want to thank you all for your work during these extenuating circumstances," Sandford began. "It's never easy to thrive under duress, but that's what we're under right now. I trust you're all aware of the current situation."

That was the last moment Sandford felt any sense of control in the meeting, for the next five minutes resembled an unmoderated *Crossfire* debate more than a room full of experts serving at the pleasure of the President. Fingers pointed, wagged and even formed crass gestures. Accusations flew around the room. Words like "coup" and "anarchy" and "unpatriotic" filled the air. This was no cabinet meeting aimed at gaining control of the situation—this was a hive of political partisanship where the worker bees were eating their own. *If I can't control the cabinet, how am I going to control this country?*

Sandford stood up and slammed his palms on the desk.

"Enough!" he screamed. The room immediately fell silent. *At least they respect anger.*

"The President asked you to serve on this cabinet, but nobody here seems to be able to do that. I suggest if you want to maintain your position here, you need to stop with these shenanigans and do what you're supposed to do: give me advice on how to proceed. Otherwise, I'll replace you with someone who will."

Sandford's control grab worked, creating a more cooperative environment. But it didn't take long before the meeting grew tenser.

"Our final item is to talk about what's going on in Russia," Sandford said. "I've read reports from Homeland Security that not only are the Russians building more missile silos in Siberia but they're also pointing some at us right now. I think we need to show them that we won't be intimidated."

Sandford's suggestion was met by some resistance, as the doves in the room pleaded against using any force, much less showing some. The hawks created an echo chamber for Sandford's idea, urging him to do what President Briggs lacked the fortitude to do. The ensuing debate caused an uproar that rivaled the early minutes of the meeting.

This time, Sandford pounded his fist on the table, quieting the room once again.

"Thank you for your input," he said. "I've made my decision. We're going to show Russia that we mean business."

With that, he thanked everyone for attending the meeting before dismissing them.

It's time somebody with some real guts led this country.

THE WARREN OMISSIONS | 153

Sandford wished he didn't need the near death of the President to gain access to his power. But such were the casualties of war. This was war, too. Sandford couldn't be convinced otherwise. Russia had been needling the U.S. for far too long and shirking any attempt at diplomatic relations. On the international stage, Russian president Ruslan Petrov made Briggs look like a fool. *Not me. They're going to wish they never picked a fight they couldn't win.*

Sandford was going to launch missiles at Russia. They were going to pay for whatever they did to his daughter.

***

DIANE DIXON EXITED THE ROOM, seething at what just happened. The Secretary of Education was not about to let President Briggs' decision to err on the side of diplomacy take a backseat to the hawkish Vice President.

She dialed a number on her cell phone as she retreated into a private office down the hall.

"We need to talk," Dixon said.

"What's going on?" the woman on the other end of the line said.

"Briggs is about to start a war with the Russians—and you're the only person who can stop it."

CHAPTER 36

FLYNN AND NATALIE made their way to the subway and headed toward Grand Central to take a train back to Washington. Unwilling to risk being apprehended, Flynn decided railway was the easiest and quickest way to escape the city. After all, he had immobilized a federal agent—and that wouldn't be looked upon too kindly, even if it did garner results.

"What's going to happen now?" Natalie asked as they stepped inside their private car on a train headed toward the nation's capital.

"You are going to find some place where the Kuklovod can't find you—I don't know—a long lost friend or a distant relative. I don't care who, but someone who isn't going to be easy to trace back to you. Understand?"

Natalie nodded. She stared out the window. The blank look on her face told Flynn the trauma of the past few days disturbed her, to say the least. *This isn't exactly the way to impress a woman. She's probably wondering if it will be like this forever.*

She wasn't the only one wondering that. Flynn tried to imagine any scenario where the Kuklovod would give up on him and just let him live his life. They had before—but that was only because he hadn't uncovered their plot to incite a war between the U.S. and Russia. Now, Flynn proved to be an even bigger liability. They couldn't just let him go get on television and broadcast such plans to the public now that he had more detailed firsthand knowledge. They would make every effort to silence him, if not for his intelligence, for murdering three of their operatives—though Flynn wondered if they were simply freelancers. Either way, he wasn't safe. And neither was Natalie.

I've got to talk to Osborne.

He dialed Osborne's number on the burner phone he purchased in the train station while waiting to board.

"Osborne."

"Osborne, it's Flynn."

Osborne's voice turned to a whisper. "Are you OK, man? Where are you?"

"We're heading back to D.C.," Flynn said.

"We? Who's with you?"

"Natalie. They took her hostage as leverage."

"Natalie? The gal from the archives?"

"Yeah, that's her." Flynn looked at Natalie and smiled. She didn't look at him, continuing to gaze out the window in a stupor.

"Are you guys dating?"

"Look, I don't want to talk about that right now. We've got more important things to discuss."

"You're telling me. Barksdale listed you as the prime suspect before I proved that you were trying to stop the assassin. Of course I knew he would be with you, but I couldn't risk some trigger-happy blockhead wanting to squeeze a round off into you because he wanted Seal Team Six fame."

"Thanks. But the assassin is still on the loose. I left a mess for you to clean up at a warehouse a few miles from the U.N. building."

"Who's the assassin?"

"Ivan. This was a Kuklovod hit."

"What else do you know?"

"I know they're trying to start a war between us and Russia."

"Tell me something I don't already know. They don't need to help that process."

"What do you mean?"

"I mean, Gerald Sandford is now the acting President and he's ready to fire the first shot, if my sources are right."

Flynn then asked Osborne if he could help hide Natalie at a CIA safe house until this whole thing settled down. They set up a time to meet and go over any other information Flynn learned.

"There's something else you need to know, Flynn."

"What's that?"

"I can't talk about it now, but I need to know something."

"Oh?"

"Are you still up for a mission?"

CHAPTER 37

IVAN SEETHED AS HE WATCHED the news from his hotel room. Three Russian terrorists were found dead in a warehouse several miles from the U.N. According to the report, law enforcement officials hadn't yet identified if they were involved in the assassination attempt on the President, but early indications showed this was likely the case.

He flipped through the television channels. He wanted a shred of good news, something that let him know his mission wasn't a waste. Though he was in critical condition, the President was still alive. His men had let his hostages escape. And no news agency reported any sign of impending war. Maybe there was still hope that something would go right.

Thirty minutes of sitting and waiting, Ivan fumed even more. James Flynn was still out there, that rock in his shoe. More like a gash on his wrist. If this plan failed to incite a war, Ivan knew it would be because of Flynn's meddling. With no other directive at the moment, he needed a diversion. *Time to make Flynn pay.* He picked up his phone and began dialing some numbers. *Time to get serious.*

CHAPTER 38

BY THE TIME FLYNN MET with Osborne on Saturday afternoon in Washington, the President's death had been erroneously reported via Twitter by three different reporters. Every newsperson worth his weight in salt wanted to be credited as the journalist who broke the news first. This race to be first trumped the race to be right, leaving the general public weary of their ridiculous games. Flynn had fallen for news of Brad Pitt's death, Jay Leno's campaign donations to the Republican party, and Miley Cyrus's decision to quit making music—the first sad, the second shocking, and the third wishful thinking. And all of it on Twitter, not a word of it true. *Where's my cynicism when I need it most?*

With plenty of rumors swirling around the Beltway over who was really running the show at the White House and who was at who's throat, only one thing seemed clear: A leadership vacuum existed. Not that this came as any surprise to Flynn—or any other American. The country had been floundering in the eyes of the international community due to its constant meddling in foreign affairs and inability to stabilize the global financial sector. Now a new drummer was thrumming for a war.

"Thanks for coming down here," Osborne said to Flynn as he shut the door to his office.

"Well, I'm curious as to what you might have in mind," Flynn said.

"Without being overly dramatic, I need you. This country needs you. The world needs you."

Flynn chuckled. "Do I look like Jesus Christ to you?"

"Save your sarcasm for later. I'm serious. There's some big stuff about to go down—and I need you to do something about it."

Flynn drummed his fingers on the desk before leaning forward to speak.

"What could I possibly do to stop this madness?"

"If you execute an off-the-books mission, the answer is *everything*."

"And what if I happen to fail?"

Osborne let Flynn's question hang in the air before answering. "I think you know."

"Are you out of your mind?"

"No, but you're the best option I've got."

"You seriously don't have any other operatives who can do this mission to *save the world?*" Flynn asked.

"Sure, I do. But none of them could pull it off. It'd be a death sentence. You on the other hand —"

"So, I've been gone from the agency for several years and you still think I'm your best option?"

"Yes."

"Playing to my ego won't work."

"If only I was simply playing to your ego. But I'm being honest. I need you like never before."

Flynn buried his head in his hands then tugged at fistfuls of his hair. He let out a low growl.

"If it works out, I know it'd make a heck of a book—though you wouldn't be allowed to actually write it," Osborne said.

Flynn looked up and glared at Osborne.

"OK, OK, I'm sorry—just a little humor. But I'm serious when I say I need you."

"Suppose I say yes. What exactly is it you want me to do?"

"Go to Russia and disarm the missiles at the Kuklovod's base camp. They are planning on launching the first salvo to incite a war—that is if Sandford doesn't launch our missiles first."

Flynn stared out the window and shook his head. He would've jumped at this chance when he was with the agency, but things felt different now. Everything about his life was different. This was what he left behind. Adrenaline. Fear. Danger. Heroism. Appearing on cable network news to discuss dark government secrets fascinated him far more than rushing into a situation that could have lethal repercussions for himself. He remained silent, lost in thought.

"If you can't do it for your country, will you at least do it for the one person who always believed in you?"

Flynn jerked his gaze back toward Osborne.

"You want me to do this for my mother?" Flynn said as he leaked a wry smile.

Osborne shook his head and smiled. Flynn was in.

"How's your Russian?"

CHAPTER 39

BETHANY BRIGGS SQUEEZED her husband's hand before leaving his side for the first time to do anything other than use the restroom since her husband was shot. The past twenty-four hours tested her faith in ways she never imagined. *Is this really happening?*

She turned the door handle before looking back at her husband lying in a coma, fighting for his life. Tears streamed down her face, smearing her mascara. She daubed her wet checks with the back of her hand, unwilling to be seen as a weak woman. Pushing past the two secret service agents guarding the door, Bethany made her way down the hall and into a private unoccupied conference room.

Bethany pulled the door shut behind her, locking it. She loved her husband—and she loved her country. And right now, if she believed everything she heard, both were in danger of vanishing as she knew them. The television in the corner of the room displayed images from the chaos interspersed with talking heads opining about the future of America's leadership or how much longer the President would live.

She pulled out her cell phone and hit redial. Even the most bull-headed of personalities struggled to say *no* to Diane Dixon. But Bethany didn't foresee any problems with the request Diane was about to make.

"So what do you want me to do?" Bethany asked, foregoing any formalities as Diane answered.

"I want you to be the acting President," Diane said.

"What? I can't do that."

"Yes, you can. Think of yourself as the second coming of Edith Wilson."

"I'm not sure I'm following you."

"When Woodrow Wilson fell ill, it was his wife Edith who kept up pretenses that her husband was still fit to run the country."

"I know the story—but Wilson wasn't in a coma. He was just partially paralyzed."

"Sure, but who's getting in to see the President these days? Anyone other than his physicians? I can be very persuasive at getting people to keep quiet."

"Can we legally do this?"

"Can you forge your husband's signature?"

"Yes."

"Then that's the answer to your question. Just don't ask me too many other questions. I need plausible deniability."

"OK, fine. What do I need to do first?"

Diane explained all the fine details to Bethany before hanging up.

Bethany wondered what her husband—a real patriot—would think about what she was about to do. *If it will stop a war, I'm sure he would understand.* She was lying to herself and she knew it. Her rationale would be defeated by the President's principled approach to following protocol and precedence. At least there was one good thing about him being in a coma.

CHAPTER 40

IVAN SQUATTED IN THE DARK, hoping his hunch was right. So far, things were going according to plan. The President was sidelined and his replacement was itching to fire missiles in the air and start the next world war.

Yet a fly in the ointment remained: James Flynn.

He had disposed of some of the world's most ruthless MI-6 agents with about as much trouble as it took him to eat a piece of cake. But not Flynn. The enigmatic journalist seemed to get the jump on him at every turn. Ivan wondered how a former CIA agent with such intuition could have left the agency so easily. As much as Ivan wanted to kill Flynn, he also strangely admired him.

Only once before had an agent challenged him, pushing him to the brink of death. On a mission to secure long-range missiles in Nepal, Ivan crossed paths with a CIA operative who somehow learned about the deal he was about to make with foreign mercenaries. Having never met his contact, Ivan set everything up in a clandestine site near a frozen lake. It was how Ivan conducted business: get what he wants, then murder the seller. Nobody came looking for these lowlifes, and even if they did, they'd be hard pressed to find them at the bottom of the lake.

But on this particular day, Ivan was the one surprised. A sniper hit him with a tranquilizer. Ivan never even saw his face. Twenty minutes later, Ivan awoke naked and gasping for air beneath a partially frozen lake. He had no idea how long he'd been underwater—or how he survived for that matter. When he resurfaced, figuring out how was the furthest thing from his mind. He wanted revenge. It was all he could think about as he warmed himself by a fire, one he found blazing with all the money he'd brought to the exchange. The sniper had laid Ivan's clothes neatly laid by the fire along with a note that read: "If I see you again, I won't be so kind."

Ivan lost a couple of toes due to frostbite he suffered during that mission, but he didn't lose his resolve. He was more determined than ever to fulfill the Kuklovod's mission, even if it meant taking out the CIA one operative at a time. Yet all his years of persistent and hard work had resulted in bringing the organization to the precipice of achieving his seemingly unattainable goal.

And everything was going to be fine once James Flynn was out of the picture.

CHAPTER 41

FLYNN RETURNED TO HIS APARTMENT to pack. He had an hour to gather his things and report to the airfield where he would fly halfway around the world and hope to accomplish a solo mission that would stave off a world war. He worried about Natalie and what might happen to her as a result of his reckless entrance into this investigation. But there was no time to let his emotions distract him. He nearly called Osborne a half dozen times on his way home, mulling over the impending disaster that would befall the U.S. if he did nothing. But his country needed him—even if it said it didn't. Osborne needed him, which trumped any vindictiveness hurled at him by the agency. As long as one person believed in him, that's all Flynn needed.

As Flynn packed, he winced. The mere thought of returning to Russia made him shudder. Bitter cold. Sketchy intel. Knives waiting to be shoved in your back. The country bred traitors like it was its top export commodity. Anything for money. Honor and valor meant nothing to anyone. It was all about getting paid. At times, such a culture played to his advantage, but a higher bidder almost always cost him. This time, he would avoid such tactics. The less prisoners, the better. He knew this was a mess even some members of the Russian government wouldn't mind cleaning up.

Flynn stuffed thermal undergarments into a duffle bag and a few gadgets he hadn't surrendered to the agency upon his dismissal. These gadgets would never make James Bond envious, but they got the job done. A remote optical camera. A shotgun mic that could pick up conversations from long distances. Even a pair of boots concealing a knife. *You never know when you might need one.* Flynn shook his head as he stared at the relics of past missions. *What are you doing? Are you out of your mind? You're an investigative reporter now, not some vigilante hero.* As quickly as the thoughts pinged around his head, he dismissed them. *Osborne needs me.*

As Flynn closed one of his drawers, he froze. A creaking noise put him on alert. Breathless, Flynn waited another moment or two. Nothing. *Must be the house settling.*

He pulled open his top drawer to fetch his final necessary item— his lucky bullet, complete with a chain around it. Flynn wore it on all his missions after a doctor retrieved it from his stomach following an incident in the Congo. Tasked with identifying the buyer of weapons dealer Joseph Kyenge's cache of long-range ballistic missiles, Flynn made a mistake during his surveillance. The sun glinted off his binoculars while he lay prostrate on a cliff above Kyenge's camp. After avoiding the initial hail of bullets, Flynn suffered a near fatal shot when one of the bullets glanced off a rock and lodged in his stomach. The agony of driving while trying to escape capture was a memory he couldn't shake. He managed to lose Kyenge's guards and found his way back to the bush plane where his pilot flew him to a village with a visiting doctor from the U.S. Flynn learned later that there were a few tense moments, but the doctor saved his life as he put together a makeshift operating room, retrieved the bullet and sutured the wound. He never found out who purchased the weapons—and it ate at him. *Those stupid binoculars.*

Flynn stared at the warped bullet in his hand. It stirred courage in him like nothing else. *Not even a bullet can stop me.* He knew he was over-stating his ability to survive such a hit, but he didn't care. If he dwelt on the reality of how close he came to dying, he might lock himself up in a room and never see the outside world again. He lived in a dangerous world for a long time, but he also knew he could just as well die in a car accident or from a heart attack going about his everyday life. Dead was dead. *Better to die doing something meaningful.*

Creeeeeeeak!

Flynn froze again. *Am I imagining things?* He waited a couple of seconds before moving.

Without warning, Flynn's closet door burst open as an assailant raced toward him. Flynn recognized him immediately—Ivan. Flynn dodged the blade being waved about. Thinking on his feet, Flynn used the bullet chain to grasp Ivan's blade-carrying hand, forcing the blade to the floor. The two exchanged blows before Ivan earned the upper hand, taking Flynn down with a swift kick to his outer shin and pouncing on top of him. Flynn struggled beneath Ivan's imposing frame.

Ivan pinned Flynn's arms to the ground and grabbed the closest object he could find—Flynn's bullet chain. He began choking Flynn. Squirming to relieve the pressure on his neck, Flynn freed his arms and jammed the fingers on his right hand beneath the chain to prevent rapid asphyxiation. With his left hand, Flynn groped underneath his bed. He kept trying to wrestle away from Ivan as he felt several items. A pair of socks. Dirty boxes. *Where is it?* Then, he found it—the cold cylindrical can of bear spray. Gasping for air, Flynn directed the spray right at Ivan, who rolled off him, clutching his eyes in pain. The agonizing yelp pierced Flynn's ears.

Flynn fished out the pistol from his bag and held it on Ivan as he kicked the knife away from him.

"Now get up!" Flynn barked.

Ivan staggered to his feet, still burying his face in his hands and whimpering from the pain.

Flynn jammed his gun into Ivan's back. "I've got a lot of questions for you—but I don't have time to ask them now. Unfortunately for you, I'm going to let someone much more unpleasant than myself ask them."

Flynn led Ivan down into the garage of his townhome and tied him to a support pole, at least eight feet away from any other object in the garage. He then proceeded to pat down Ivan and search for any other objects that might assist him in cutting himself free. Satisfied that Ivan was devoid of any chance at escape, Flynn shook his head as he looked at Ivan.

"The press is going to have a field day with you," Flynn said.

Ivan spit at him and then hung his head.

Unbothered by Ivan's gesture, Flynn headed up stairs and turned the lights out.

He locked the door as his cell phone buzzed.

"Where are you?" Osborne demanded after Flynn answered.

"I've been a little busy."

Osborne didn't seem interested in Flynn's excuse.

"We don't have any time to waste. Get down to the airfield now."

"Sorry, I was just busying apprehending the President's assassin. You can thank me later."

Osborne stopped panicking.

"You did *what?*"

"You heard me. Ivan jumped me in my house and tried to kill me. But I left him for you in my garage. Send someone over here quick to pick him up."

"Good work. Now hurry up! You've got a war to stop!"

CHAPTER 42

GERALD SANDFORD WATCHED the activity swirling around his office. In just a few short hours, he would unleash his pent-up fury on Russia for taking his daughter from him. Though it was a different kind of taking than he initially believed. Sydney wasn't dead—and he hoped she wouldn't become a pawn in this high-stakes game. But he was going to make sure Russia paid for whatever part they played in her disappearance from his life for the past 15 years.

One of the speech writers thrust a document into his hands, hoping to gain the acting President's approval on the diatribe just written for the American public—and for its number one enemy. While Briggs played to the whims of the American people, Sandford refused any such notions. *I'm going to show this country what it means to lead.* He scanned the speech, one that conveyed his resolve to remove Americans from the threat imposed by another nation, subtly hinting that his country was about to take its rightful place as the world's leading superpower.

An aide tapped Sandford on the shoulder.

"Mr. President, I have something that I think you should read."

Sandford spun around, brow furrowed as he looked up at the timid young man.

"What is it?" Sandford demanded.

"Diane Dixon has requested an emergency cabinet meeting."

"What would possess her to request such a thing now?"

"Apparently, President Briggs has made a miraculous recovery."

"Say *what?*" Sandford grew enraged. "How is that even possible?"

"I'm not sure, but I've got a letter right here signed by President Briggs himself that he's fit to lead and is requesting to be reinstated immediately."

Sandford shook his head. *No, no, no! I am the President now! This isn't happening!*

He looked back up at the aide and nodded. "Set it up."

Sandford needed some time to plot his next move. He wasn't going to relinquish power this easily.

CHAPTER 43

FIFTEEN MINUTES AFTER LEAVING HIS HOUSE, Flynn's phone buzzed. It was Osborne again, demanding to know where he was.

"If you're not a 'what have you done for me lately' kind of guy, nobody is," Flynn answered. "I called you a few minutes ago to tell you that I apprehended the President's assassin and now I'm getting drilled for being late. What is it with you government people?"

Osborne didn't appreciate the joke.

"This is serious, Flynn. We need to be wheels up in five minutes."

"Well, good. I'm only two minutes away. Have you got to my house yet?"

"Nope. I sent some agents there ahead of me. I should hear something soon."

"Good. Keep me posted. I'd love to know if there's something you can get out of him that will help me on this mission."

"There's only one thing you need to know—shoot to kill. We'll send in a team to clean up the mess after you get control of those missiles."

"Isn't Sandford going to shoot first?"

"I hope not. And if he doesn't, the Kuklovod is ready to ignite this powder keg with their own special flare. It's why we need you to get there quickly."

Flynn hung up as he pulled into the hangar. He parked and got out of his car. He grabbed his bag and hustled toward the plane's open door.

Before he got on the plane, a CIA handler shoved a file folder into

Flynn's hands and began giving him a quick rundown of the highlights and protocol for the mission.

The handler, a woman in her late 20s, looked Flynn up and down and then smiled. She appeared feisty. Flynn thought maybe she was eyeing him.

"Is this how you handle all your assets?" Flynn asked, trying not to enjoy her attention. "I'm not a piece of meat, you know."

"I didn't think you were," she shot back. "I was just wondering how cold you'd be when you jump out of this plane."

Mouth gaping, Flynn stared at her.

"Did you just say what I think you said?" he asked.

"You didn't think we were going to touch down at the local airport and just stroll into the Kuklovod's headquarters, now, did you?" She shot him a wink before adding, "Good luck, conspiracy man. Better you than me."

With that, she gave Flynn a little shove toward the plane and started walking away.

Flynn began a mild protest. "Osborne never said anything about jumping out of a plane. This has got to be some kind of mistake."

"Let's go," barked one of the co-pilots standing at the top of the plane's stairs.

Flynn continued to look stunned.

"Osborne knows I hate heights," he muttered to himself.

"Buckle up," the co-pilot said as he prepared to enter the cabin. "It's going to be a long and bumpy ride."

Flynn slumped into the chair and stretched out his legs before buckling his seat belt. He hung his head in disbelief at the revelation that his exit from the jet wouldn't be the conventional way. *If Osborne was here right now …*

Flynn's phone started buzzing. It was Osborne.

"Why you little jerk!" Flynn answered, despite Osborne trying to say something. Flynn just kept talking over him. "You said nothing to me about jumping out of a plane. You know how I hate heights."

When Flynn finally took a breath, Osborne broke in.

"Will you just shut up for a minute and listen to me?" Osborne said.

"What is it?"

"It's Ivan. I'm at your house—and he's gone."

"Don't worry. He won't get far."

CHAPTER 44

WHEN GERALD SANDFORD WALKED into the cabinet meeting, the room roared with raised voices. Finger pointing, head wagging, and fist pounding dominated the non-verbal communication. He didn't need to hear an actual word being said. *Ain't democracy great?* He sneered as he surveyed the room before choosing his next words.

"Quiet!" Sandford said as he walked toward his chair. "Everyone sit down and shut up!"

He relished the moment. The room was littered with people he dreamed about putting in their place one day. Now he was the President. Who cared what little stunt Diane Dixon was trying to pull? This was going to be a bare-knuckled street brawl if necessary. And he wasn't about to pull a single punch.

With the room silenced, Sandford finally addressed everyone.

"We're here today because Diane Dixon has learned that the President has somehow made a remarkable recovery in such a short period of time and is now fit to lead—and that he was never unfit. She wants all my actions declared void over the last 24 hours, claiming that we skirted constitutional rules in promoting me in an acting capacity for the office of the President.

"But let me be clear about one thing: I'm happy to relinquish the chair as long as I know the President is fully coherent and making his own decisions instead of being a puppet for his closest advisors. I will not stand for such treason and will make every effort to strike down any such attempts.

"With that said, Ms. Dixon, you have the floor."

Sandford sat down in his chair and leaned forward, hands clasped in front of him. He felt powerful and he wanted to look that way. More than anything, he wanted to intimidate anybody who thought they could dupe him out of a position that desperately required genuine leadership at the moment. *Briggs would be squirming in this seat if he were here right now, asking everybody what he should do and never coming up with an idea on his own. Pathetic.* It was what Sandford detested most about Briggs. Ultimately, it was what got Briggs elected. Plenty of special interest groups delighted in the opportunity to pull the strings in Washington. It was the same game U.S. Presidents had been playing for years, kowtowing to those who helped put them in office. They cared little about their accomplishments but about being the most powerful man in the free world for eight years. Sandford knew the real power rested elsewhere, but at the moment, the power that accompanied the presidency was all he wanted. He needed that seat to pay back the Russians, maybe he even save his daughter.

For the next twenty minutes, Diane shared what she knew and fielded objections from the cabinet. She managed to convince enough of the cabinet that President Briggs was fit enough to lead, forcing a motion to vote on his reinstatement. She needed a majority to make it happen—and the vote finished tied. Sandford was asked to break the vote.

"Well, it seems like we've got quite a predicament here," Sandford began. "You know I'd be happy to give this chair back to Arthur Briggs if he's truly fit to lead. However, I'm not going to take the word of some letter. I want to know that's he functioning on his own. I'll need to take a visit to see him and talk it through. If I'm satisfied that he's well enough to continue leading, I'll give him his chair back. But until then, I'm going to have to decline to begin the reinstatement process."

Diane stood up and defiantly smacked the table with the healthy-sized folder in her hands.

"You're making a mockery out of the system," Diane said. "And here I thought that you were a patriot."

Sandford then stood too. He pointed his finger at her as he responded.

"Oh, no. Don't think you're going to get away with that on me," he said. "If there's anyone trying to make a mockery out of the system, it's you, Ms. Dixon. I'll bet this signature isn't even the President's. You probably got someone to forge it. In fact, I'm going to take this to a handwriting expert to be analyzed. You better pray this is real or I'm coming after you with everything I've got."

Diane stormed out of the room, which erupted into another noisy argument upon her exit.

Sandford seethed as he sat in his chair. He didn't know how smart of an idea it was to call her bluff—especially if she wasn't bluffing. But none of that mattered. He merely bought himself a little bit more time to get everything together to attack Russia. It wouldn't be long now.

He exited the room and pulled out his cell phone.

"Get me General Hill. We need to discuss launch procedures."

CHAPTER 45

IVAN LOCKED HIMSELF in the special needs restroom at the Ronald Reagan Washington National Airport. He hated the airport, mostly because of who it was named after. If the world loathed Hitler, true communists equally detested Reagan. The Kuklovod saw his time as President as a promising opportunity to spark a world war, but Andropov and Chernenko lacked the fortitude to strike first. And so did Reagan. It was an era of posturing for the public—a chance considered wasted by the Kuklovod. Ivan found sadistic irony in the fact that this particular airport would serve as his port of departure.

He sifted through the handful of passports in his hand, trying to decide who he would be before he matched his hairstyle to the selected passport. *Ezekiel Egwu. Perfect.* Ivan would play the part of a British Nigerian anthropology professor going to do work on the Khanty people in the Urals. Egwu was his favorite alias since it required a dreadlocks wig—and in this case, it made the most sense as a cover.

He affixed his wig and put on his thick black glasses for a more scholarly appearance. It was time to escape this country, a place he detested for how it arrogantly squandered its wealth and power on meaningless things. *They will soon learn what's most important in life.* He smiled at the thought. It was time to find a flight and buy a ticket.

Still remaining in the confines of the spacious restroom, Ivan purchased a ticket for Paris that was leaving in less than an hour. From Paris, it would be easy to slip back into Russia without much scrutiny. He then gathered his belongings and headed to the ticket counter where he picked up his boarding pass and headed toward the security checkpoint.

He passed through the identification checkpoint before merging into another slow-moving line that required the removal of his shoes, coat, belt and any other object deemed to have the ability to conceal a weapon. Ivan enjoyed listening to the stories of old by Kuklovod veterans who reminisced about the days when you could carry a knife or a gun on board without even getting checked. Getting examined closely was a hassle he could do without, though watching those American towers melt to the ground on September 11th made the hassle worth it to him. Yet that was child's play compared to the fury the Kuklovod was set to unleash on American soil.

While standing in line, Ivan's phone rang. It was his supervisor. Ivan spoke in Russian to mask the conversation.

"I'll be there in twenty-four hours," Ivan said.

"Did you eliminate the threat?" the man asked.

"Not completely, but I will."

The next minute consisted of a dressing down. Ivan listened patiently as his supervisor hurled every imaginable insult at him. He didn't even say good-bye before abruptly hanging up.

Ivan's supervisor shouted so loudly that those around Ivan began to stare at him, wondering what the nature of the conversation could be about. The fellow travelers appeared uneasy and Ivan sensed it immediately. Some travelers whispered to one another, staring at Ivan. It was evident that the phone call caused a scene, both in the nature of the call and in the language foreign to everyone around him.

Ivan hung up, looking sheepish for the benefit of those around him. He hoisted his backpack and other belongings up onto the X-ray belt. Inwardly, Ivan fumed, angry that he let Flynn get the best of him. It was one score he hoped to settle if he ever saw Flynn again.

"Sir, will you please come with me?" the TSA agent asked Ivan.

Lost in a stupor, Ivan jolted back to reality.

"Me? Did I do something wrong?" Ivan asked.

"Just step this way, sir."

The TSA agent ushered Ivan to a private room located off the back of the security checkpoint area. He then closed the door.

"I need you to remove all your outer garments so we can do a proper search."

"What do you mean?" Ivan asked incredulously.

"I mean, take off all your clothes except for your underwear. We found something of a suspicious nature and need to investigate."

Ivan reluctantly complied, grumbling about the American government under his breath in Russian.

"Is that what you really think about America?" the TSA agent asked.

Ivan looked up stunned. He rarely ran into any Americans who knew Russian, much less some low-level hourly employee like this one.

The agent radioed for extra help in the room.

"What are you doing?" Ivan demanded.

"Sir, you need to calm down and chill out. I have a partner coming in here to join me and make sure you don't get out of control."

"I'm not out of control," Ivan said, raising his voice.

"I think you just need to have a seat, sir."

Ivan plopped into a chair, humiliated. First, his supervisor. Now, some low life TSA agent. Nothing was going right for him at the moment. *Just calm down. It will be all right.*

Another TSA agent entered the room, one who appeared to be more important than the man who ushered Ivan into the room. Ivan noted how he spoke with more confidence and with more authority. He then turned to Ivan.

"We found this on you, sir," the TSA supervisor said, producing an odd pocket knife. "Are you aware that federal regulations prohibit passengers from carrying a blade of this length?"

Ivan had never seen the pocketknife in his life, and wondered if he'd been set up by a passenger or was getting duped by the TSA. Either way, it was apparent that he needed to remain calm if he was going to escape the situation.

"It has the initials J.F. inscribed on the blade," the supervisor said again.

"Oh, yes," Ivan said, after a few silent moments. "It's a knife from my mother's father—an heirloom passed down. I'm an anthropologist and those things are important to me. It was terribly clumsy of me not to pack it in my luggage."

184 | R.J. PATTERSON

The two TSA personnel stared at each other for a moment before the supervisor finally spoke.

"Look, we normally just confiscate contraband like this, but since it's an heirloom, I'll let you fill out one of these envelopes here and mail it back to your home address. You OK with that?"

Ivan nodded.

He took the package, a pen, and the knife from the supervisor and began scribbling down James Flynn's address with his own name at the top. He stuffed the knife inside and sealed it before handing it back to the supervisor.

"Thank you very much, sir," Ivan said. "I appreciate your kindness and understanding. I won't let that happen again."

"Have a nice flight," the supervisor said and motioned toward the door with his hand.

Ivan quickly redressed and collected his things before leaving the room. *Unbelievable. I'm gonna kill that James Flynn the next chance I get.*

Luck seemed to be on Ivan's side, even when it didn't first appear so.

He smiled as he headed down the concourse. *Let's go start a war.*

CHAPTER 46

FLYNN ENJOYED FLYING in the CIA's jets, if only for their extensive luxuries. Plush leather seats, a fully stocked bar, flat screen televisions. "If only there was a football game on," Flynn mused. But then, he couldn't be distracted by such diversions. With a war looming between two of the world's most powerful nations, nothing was more important than his mission.

But this wasn't just another CIA jet. This was the Lockheed Martin QSST (Quiet Supersonic Transport) prototype capable of speeds beyond 1,200 miles per hour. According to Osborne, this one was on loan to the CIA for testing purposes, registered to a French billionaire who also happened to be an agency asset. And today it was the only aircraft that could get Flynn near the Kuklovod headquarters, nestled in the Ural mountains, by early Sunday morning.

The plane's phone rang, prompting Flynn to answer it. It was Osborne.

"Are you clear about the mission?"

"I think so," Flynn answered. "But just to be clear, I'm in this on my own—right? Like, there's no cavalry coming if I get caught and you'll disavow any knowledge of me?"

"You got it. This one is completely off the books. The only people who know what you're doing are the pilots, Lauren and me."

"Lauren?"

"Sure, the sassy handler you met at the hangar? I'm sure you remember her."

"Oh, yes, how could I forget? She's the one who told me that I'm going to be jumping out of this plane."

"Well, yes, I was hoping you were over that, but apparently you're not."

"Geez, Osborne. You know how I feel about jumping out of a perfectly good aircraft."

"Oh, I know. But would you have agreed to go if I told you ahead of time?"

"OK, I get your point—but that doesn't mean I'm forgiving you anytime soon."

"Fine. Whatever. Just as long as you stop the Kuklovod."

"What's the story in Washington?"

"Sandford is pressing hard to strike the Russians first, while a faction of the President's cabinet is trying to get him reinstated."

"Reinstated? Is President Briggs fine now?"

"Not from what I've heard, but you never can be sure about the rumors bantered about in the Beltway."

Osborne paused.

"Listen, Flynn. There's something else you need to know about this mission."

"Yeah? What?"

"There's another variable to take into consideration."

"What variable?"

"A variable named Sydney Sandford."

"Sydney Sandford? I thought she was dead. What are you suggesting?"

"We all did. But I think part of what's fueling Sandford's rage to strike back at the Russians is a picture he received of Sydney providing proof of life."

"Well, he's always hated the Russians. That's never been a secret, yet the fact that she may still be alive is an interesting development. But do you believe Sandford is willing to start a war over this?"

"Maybe—I can't be sure of anything except that his hatred is stoked by his bitterness over losing his daughter in Russia and how he perceived that they never lifted a finger to help return her dead body—or as we now know, locate her. But I'm not sure what's going on with him. He's a loose cannon. And Sydney may be with these guys. They may use her as a bargaining chip—you just never know. So be careful, OK?"

"You know me."

"I do—that's why I said 'be careful.' "

Flynn laughed and shook his head before hanging up. Osborne knew him better than anyone—and it's why Flynn could handle his personal comments, snide or otherwise. No one else had earned the right to say things in jest like Osborne had. No one.

Flynn checked his watch. It was another couple of hours before he would need to suit up for the Urals' bitter October weather, where winter had fallen already.

***

ONE HOUR BEFORE THE DROP, Flynn awoke and began checking his gear. He didn't want to leave anything to chance, particularly when he was jumping out of an airplane. He only trusted himself to properly pack his chute.

Once he secured everything he needed, he checked his watch again. Fifteen minutes to the drop. He felt the jet turn nose down. The plane was to make a descent at 1.6 Mach from sixty-thousand feet to three-thousand feet above ground level (AGL), then slow momentarily to 200 knots so Flynn could make a safe exit from the aircraft. The co-pilot then shouted out a ten-minute warning.

Suddenly, the plane went into a violent 5G turn. Flynn was plastered to his seat.

"What's going on up there?" Flynn shouted toward the pilots.

"Looks like we've got company," the commanding pilot answered.

"What? Are you kidding me?"

"I wish I was jumping out. AWACS says we have two MIG-35s closing fast from our six o'clock. They will be in missile range in fifteen miles. We've got three minutes."

Flynn started to panic. *Three minutes! This wasn't supposed to happen!*

The pilot completed his evasive maneuver, and Flynn unbuckled and ran to the cockpit and seated himself in the jump seat just behind the pilots. He donned his jump helmet and secured his parachute, except for the leg straps. He watched the command pilot order the co-pilot to employ the radar jamming equipment. Flynn noticed the co-pilot reached for the switch but did not actually take the switch out of "standby." Something wasn't right. The command pilot was busy employing flares and chaff.

It was still dark but the oblivious co-pilot had not extinguished the position lights. *Is he trying to get us killed?* Flynn reached for the Glock 26 he had stashed in his leg holster, but not before the co-pilot shot the command pilot in the chest with a small pistol drawn from his coat pocket. The co-pilot then turned to take care of Flynn. He was too late. Flynn shot first—and with precision. He stared vacantly at the two lifeless bodies in the cockpit.

With both pilots dead and the jet in a supersonic dive, Flynn could only react. He unbuckled the command pilot and slung him into the jump seat. He then buckled himself into the left seat and reached across the dead co-pilot to switch on the jamming pod and kill the running lights. Descending to eight-thousand feet, the jet's GPS indicated they were in the target area. Flynn pulled the power to idle and banked the aircraft into a spiraling 5G nose down dive. This would slow the aircraft to a safe speed for jumping.

Flynn watched as the airspeed bled off and the altitude wound down. The air battle manager from AWACS called out a missile launch and the radar warning equipment chirped and blinked, indicating there had been a missile fired at the QSST. Flynn estimated one minute until impact. He hoped the evasive maneuvers would cause the missiles to miss their mark.

At two-hundred knots and three-thousand feet AGL, Flynn rolled out and leveled off. He set the automatic pilot, unbuckled, and scrambled for the emergency exit.

As Flynn got up to leave the cockpit, he noticed the co-pilot's phone buzzing with a new text message. It was from someone named "Livingston." *I knew that guy wasn't a real cop.*

He forced open the hatch and jumped into the cold night air. The first missile did miss. Flynn almost yanked at the ripcord but remembered his leg straps were not buckled. The 180 mile per hour wind caused him to tumble as he fumbled for the leg straps. It only took ten terror-stricken seconds to secure them, but it felt much longer than that to Flynn. He then assumed the free fall position, stabilizing the tumbling before pulling the ripcord. He welcomed the swift jolt as the chute opened.

Flynn had just enough time to lower the clear visor on his jump helmet before his body was pounded with tree branches rushing toward him. He came to an abrupt stop and yo-yoed a few times, suspended about eight feet off the ground in a tree. Nothing seemed to be broken. In the distance the second missile found its mark.

"I wasn't going to land that bird anyhow," Flynn muttered to himself.

It was like a magic trick where the magician focuses the audience's attention in one direction only to be pulling a sleight of hand move in the other. He couldn't ask for a more covert landing—if he absolutely had to jump from an airplane into the Urals. He experienced the most peaceful few minutes he'd had in the past few days as he lowered himself out of the tree.

Once he hit the ground, he pulled out his satellite phone and dialed Osborne. Flynn filled him in about the dramatic moments over the past few minutes.

"I never said saving the world would be easy," Osborne quipped.

Flynn growled. "I'd like to punch you in the mouth right now. Do you know that?"

Osborne laughed. "How about I just buy you a beer when you get back?"

"Make it two," Flynn said.

Osborne then went over a few more details with Flynn regarding the extraction.

"Wait a minute—I thought you said nobody knew about this mission except for the two pilots, you and Lauren. What about this extraction team?"

"Settle down, Flynn. They don't know yet, but I'm about to fill them in soon enough. I don't want to take any chances that news of your presence might leak out to anyone."

"Too late for that," Flynn said.

"Why?" Osborne asked.

Flynn started running. Gunfire filled the night air—branches were

190 | R.J. PATTERSON

being clipped off all around him as he zigged and zagged through the trees.

"Somebody already knows I'm here."

CHAPTER 47

"I'M THE PRESIDENT of the United States of America! You better give me a better answer than that!" Sandford growled.

General Timothy Hill of the U.S. Air Force refused to acquiesce to Sandford's demands.

"I'm sorry, President Sandford, but we can't skirt protocol. Our intelligence has not shown an imminent threat coming out of Russia, despite what reports you may have read. Is it possible the Russians could fire missiles at us? Yes. Is it likely based on the activity we're seeing around known Russian military sites? No."

Sandford grew more incensed by the moment.

"Get your head out of the sand, General. I looked at satellite photos last week that showed covert Russian bases preparing to launch missiles toward the U.S. They are building silos all along Siberia at a rapid rate."

"I might have my head in the sand, but launching missiles at Russia isn't as simple as getting a few launch codes," Gen. Hill replied. Then he got snippy. "With all due respect, sir, perhaps you've watched too many Tom Clancy movies."

If Sandford had been a missile, he would've detonated and destroyed half of Washington. He ran off a string of expletives that effectively ended any cordial conversation. When Sandford finished, Hill said nothing.

"When I call back tomorrow, you better have those launch codes for me," Sandford demanded.

"If you call back tomorrow, sir, maybe we can schedule a meeting with some of the other officers here at the Strategic Command. Your

192 | R.J. PATTERSON

demands aren't unreasonable if you can divulge some intelligence that we haven't seen. But for now, we're going to stick with the protocol."

Sandford slammed the phone down. It had been a tumultuous Saturday afternoon that now spilled late into Saturday night.

This wasn't how it was supposed to go. *I'm the President! People are supposed to do what I say!*

Instead, Sandford found that he wasn't surrounded by *yes* men and women. Maybe they were when President Briggs sat in the chair, but not now. Allegiances ran deep to the man who appointed them to their positions. Briggs wasn't for inciting a war—and neither were they.

Sandford had to figure out a way to change things in his favor.

He picked up the phone and called one of his advisors.

"Jim, who do we know over at Strategic Command? We need to see about relieving a certain General Hill of his duties."

CHAPTER 48

FLYNN SCRAMBLED UP A STEEP HILL, seeking cover from the soldiers stalking him in the rugged terrain of the Urals. His fingers grew numb from the bold cold air—and he'd only been there less than thirty minutes.

Finding refuge in a cave partially blocked by two large boulders, Flynn found the perfect location to put his long-range sniper skills to use. He quickly set up his rifle's tripod before putting on his night vision goggles. In his first survey of the valley below, he picked up four soldiers heading toward him. It was easy to detect even the mildest heat from the thick cold that blanketed the area.

They stopped shooting in his direction, but they were still coming. Flynn did what he was trained to do—eliminate the targets. One by one, he fired long-range shots at the oncoming soldiers, dropping them without as much as a yelp.

After the four victims disappeared into the valley brush, Flynn waited, scanning the area for more enemy fire. At least three miles away, large flames from the CIA's downed QSST jet leapt skyward. A patrol helicopter roared overhead, shining spotlights down into the valley. It hovered in an area for a few moments before moving on. Flynn held his breath, hoping the search party wouldn't see the soldiers he'd picked off. They didn't. In a matter of minutes, the helicopter vanished over the closest ridge.

Flynn waited for a few more minutes. Silence. He then fished his phone out of pocket to call Osborne.

"You still alive?" Osborne asked as he answered Flynn's call.

"Barely," Flynn said.

"Did you get shot?"

"No. I'm fine."

"Thank goodness. Are you still up for the mission?"

"Yeah, but so much for a stealthy entry and the element of surprise."

"Oh, you still have all of those when it comes to the Kuklovod. You've just got two groups who will be trying to kill you now—the Kuklovod *and* the Russian government."

"Are you *trying* to get me killed?"

"No, of course not. I'm trying to get you to stop a war."

"Well, I almost single-handedly started one tonight."

"Look, just stick with the plan and you'll be fine."

"Roger that. I'll check back once I'm all set up."

Flynn ended the call and slipped the phone back into his pocket. Nothing was going as he envisioned it. But it never really did.

He surveyed the valley one more time, confirming it was clear. After jamming his gear into his pack, Flynn shoved his pistol into the back of his pants.

As Flynn rose to get up, he slumped back to the ground, thanks to a swift knee in his back. He rolled over only to find a gun pointed at his head. His own gun was removed and cast aside as he heard the metal clank against rocks several few away.

"Don't move, cowboy," came the husky voice from the person brooding over him. It was the voice of a woman.

Flynn froze, raising his hands in surrender. He squinted to get a better look at her face but couldn't make out much under the moonless sky.

"Who are you and what do you want?" he asked, slowly sitting up.

"No, no, no. I ask the questions and you do the answering. So— who are you and what are you doing here?"

Flynn tempered his response. "I'm an American here on a hunting expedition in the Urals."

The woman laughed. "Really? I didn't know American hunters came here to shoot Russians. This must be a new thing I haven't heard of before."

That laugh. It sounded so familiar to Flynn, like he knew to whom it belonged.

"Lexie? Is that you?" he finally asked.

"James? James Flynn?"

Once the two realized they weren't combatants but friends, the tone of the conversation changed. The woman lowered her weapon.

Lexie Martin once ran missions with Flynn when they were both in the CIA, but Lexie left the agency a year before he did. Tired of the agency's grind, she took a job with a private security firm that guarded tech secrets for global companies. When a company suspected corporate espionage might be happening, Lexie uncovered the mole while guarding whatever secrets remained. She loved the new job so much that she tried to coerce Flynn to join her. He refused but stayed in touch, running in to her on occasion over the next year while on various missions.

Flynn struggled to say no to her. She had long dark hair, sultry lips, and piercing blue eyes. Beautiful enough to earn a second look but not so much as to attract the wrong kind of attention.

The two exchanged an awkward handshake that morphed into an even more awkward hug. Flynn wasn't sure he was initiating or if she was. Nevertheless, it served as an even stranger beginning to their subsequent conversation, despite the fact that Lexie almost killed him.

"I thought you left the agency?" Lexie asked.

"I didn't really leave—it left me," Flynn said.

"So, what are you doing here?"

"It's classified."

"It's classified? How can it be classified when you're not even with the agency any more?"

"Trust me, it is."

"Well, how about I declassify it for you since I know why you're here."

"What do you mean?"

"I mean, I know what you're up to. I'm guessing Osborne has you on some off-the-books mission to single-handedly take out the Kuklovod's command center since it took the CIA long enough to figure out where it was."

Flynn strained to see her piercing blue eyes but couldn't make them

196 | R.J. PATTERSON

out in the thick darkness still awaiting dawn's first ray of light.

"How do *you* know about the Kuklovod? I never even heard about them until a few weeks ago."

"Yeah, well, they've been around a while—but I didn't learn about them until I had a client ask me to track down the bastards who stole a shipment of their long-range missiles. Turns out, it was the Kuklovod."

"Wait a minute. I thought you worked for a private security firm."

"I did. But I've moved on. I was getting bored."

"So you're working for some arms dealer now?"

"Kind of. More like an arms broker."

"Is that what you're doing here? Trying to get your weapons back?"

"Yes, I am. And maybe I'll get you to help me do it."

"I can't do that, Lexie. I've got orders."

"It wouldn't be the first time you went off script. Now grab your stuff. We've got to hike out of here before daybreak."

CHAPTER 49

GERALD SANDFORD BARELY SLEPT more than thirty minutes at a time. His mind raced with the endless possibilities of what might happen in the coming days—both to his country and to his family. Fear turned to anger turned to disgust. It was a cycle that ran on repeat in his mind until the first light of day struck his bedroom window.

He crept out of bed so as to not wake his wife and went to brew himself a pot of coffee. With the way things had been going, he considered spiking it with vodka. Sunday usually meant peace and quiet, but he suspected he wouldn't sniff either of those two ideals today—or maybe for quite some time.

His coffee pot sputtered, spitting out the last remaining drops of its brew before signaling its completion with a steamy hiss. Sandford poured a cup and sat down to clear his head for just a moment. Then his phone buzzed.

"What's taking you so long?" asked the man on the other end. "I thought we had an agreement."

Caught off guard, Sandford stammered through his answer. "I—I am working on it. It's complicated."

"Well, our guy made it a lot less complicated for you by making you President. Now it's time for you to uphold your end of the bargain … that is, if you ever want to see your daughter alive again."

Sandford grew enraged.

"Now you listen here. If you as much as touch a hair on her head—"

"What? You're gonna do what? Come and get me? Promise death

197

and destruction to my entire family?" The man laughed. "You're so pathetic. No, you are going to listen to me. If I don't see missiles in the air within the next twenty-four hours, I'm going to take care of things my way. And I can promise you that you won't like how I take care of things. Do *you* understand *me*?"

Sandford nodded, too scared to speak.

"I know you're nodding, but I need to hear you say it."

Sandford mumbled a yes before jumping up from his chair and looking around the room. He headed straight for the window with the clearest vantage point into his house and searched for someone who might be watching him. Nothing. The street was quiet and vacant. His eyes shifted back and forth again as he contemplated how his every movement might be visible to someone he believed to be thousands of miles away.

"I'm glad we're clear. So, missiles in the air within twenty-four hours or else Sydney dies."

The line went dead.

Sandford fell into his chair and tried to hold his coffee. He couldn't. His unsteady hands led to a hot stream of coffee boring through his bathrobe and into his skin. He set the mug down and buried his head in his hands—and wept. It was bad enough to lose Sydney once. Now he was going to lose her all over again unless he found a way to launch those missiles and start another war.

He promised himself he would find a way.

CHAPTER 50

TODD OSBORNE LOATHED THE TERM "going dark." He preferred "flying blind" because that's what his agents were doing. In the meantime, Osborne was left in the dark, wondering what was happening, wondering if he'd ever see a particular "agent" alive again. It proved to be a legitimate fear on more occasions than he cared to recall. He hoped Flynn was up to the task—and that he hadn't gone dark just yet.

Osborne's last communication with Flynn came hours ago when he learned the QSST had been shot down by the Russians and that his asset on the ground was located by a team of soldiers, probably Russian military—though he couldn't be sure. Every rebel faction acted like they owned the country, even if it was just a sliver of land in the godforsaken Ural Mountains. But if air support was involved, it was likely the Russian government. He just hoped all his precautions to keep the plane from being traced back to the U.S. worked.

Domestically, Osborne felt like he was juggling chainsaws as he tried to keep Sandford from blasting off a few missiles at Russia. The rumors of dissention among President Briggs' cabinet had begun circulating among intelligence circles in Washington. It was only a matter of time before something drastic and bad happened. If Sandford let things get too personal, it was going to be a mess.

Osborne's phone buzzed. *Speak of the devil.* It was Sandford.

"Hello, Mr. President. What can I do for you?"

"I need your help and I need it fast."

"Slow down. What's wrong?"

"I got another call from somebody in Russia and they're going to kill Sydney if I don't launch missiles in the next twenty-four hours."

"Sir, are you sure about this?" Osborne hoped it wasn't as bad as it sounded.

"Sure as I've ever been. They even texted me a picture of Sydney after I hung up. It was awful."

"Would you mind sending it to me, sir? Perhaps we can analyze it and figure out where they are and then send an extraction team in to rescue your daughter."

"There's not enough time. I just need to figure out a way to get someone at Strategic Command to see things my way."

"Well, before you take those drastic measures, let me say this—don't ever underestimate what the CIA can do. Send me that picture and I'll see what we can do. We've got assets in play in Russia right now."

"You do? What for?"

"We have people everywhere all the time—you know that."

"Are you running some black ops mission you're not telling me about? I'm the President of the United States—you better tell me if you are."

Osborne gritted his teeth and lied. "If I was doing anything like that, sir, you'd be the first to know. Just don't do anything rash, OK. It's never good to let our emotions get the best of us. We'll find a way to get your daughter back."

Sandford said goodbye before ending the call.

Osborne flung his phone down on his desk and wondered if this plan had any chance of succeeding. He suddenly felt more burdened, as if the two situations that could lead to or avert a new world war were under his purview. And in both cases, he was now in the dark.

CHAPTER 51

THE PIERCING NOISE AWOKE FLYNN with a jolt as he rolled off the couch and hit the ground with a thud. His body barely felt the pain. It was nothing compared to his rigorous two-hour hike over the Urals' unforgiving terrain under the guise of night. Lexie Martin might have turned into a mercenary, but she was still the best at navigating dicey situations. Somehow he now awoke in her cramped apartment at the edge of the city—and she hadn't killed him in the middle of the night. Yet Flynn only fell asleep after he set up a very short perimeter alarm with one of his geeky gadgets in his pack. He still didn't trust her.

Beep! Beep! Beep! Beep! Beep! The alarm pierced the air.

Flynn looked upward and saw Lexie's body looming over him. She shook her head as she looked down at him.

"What a mess! Scared of me, Flynn? I can't believe the world's best espionage agency couldn't get anyone better to do the job."

For years, Flynn suffered endless chiding from Lexie. She appeared to find some sick pleasure in mocking him. The fact that he owed her his life after the incident the night before made her even more insufferable.

Flynn groaned before hiding his eyes from her stare and the sun's glare.

"You really are pathetic. There's no way you're going to thwart any plans the Kuklovod has."

Tired of her incessant sniping, Flynn fought back.

"Tell that to their team in New York that tried to assassinate the President."

"Wait, did they shoot the President? And you're going to claim responsibility for stopping it just because he's still on life support in some hospital? I'm sure you'll get a nice thank you card from the First Lady for leaving her with an invalid to take care of for the rest of her life."

Flynn started to respond and then stopped. It wasn't worth it. It never was with Lexie. Her sharp-witted and often bitter tongue always left him overmatched. She would always believe herself to be superior. If he leaped a tall building in a single bound, she would explain it away or tell you about a time she leaped two tall buildings with only an hour of sleep the night before while capturing two of the three most elusive criminals in the world. The story would drag on about how incompetent the CIA was and if it wasn't for her saving them from their own incompetence, they likely wouldn't still exist. While mildly annoying, Flynn often enjoyed hearing her braggadocios claims. Lexie's creativity impressed him the most.

"So what are we going to do?" Flynn finally said.

"We're going to go get my missiles back—and you're going to go back to the States as the hero who dismantled the Kuklovod."

Lexie moved several feet away to the kitchen and began cooking a large omelet while she shared her objectives.

Flynn protested. "I'm not sure I'm on board with that plan." He sat down in the kitchen, eyeing her every move.

"Which part? The hero part? Yeah, you're right. Nobody would believe it. We should probably just amend that to you'll be going back to the States in one piece."

Flynn sighed. "Do you have to be so nasty all the time?"

"I'm not being nasty—I'm just being truthful. Do you seriously think America is going to lap up some story about their beloved conspiracy theorist saving them from the brink of war? Please."

"They buy most of the war-time hero stories they are fed by the military."

"Yeah, but that's different. Those are soldiers. You know, people trained to kill enemies and protect us."

Flynn tried not to let her get under his skin. He didn't want to get too snippy until he had some of Lexie's omelet on his plate. He eyed her carefully as she split it apart and served it onto two separate dishes.

Flynn knew how she could get if he fought back too hard.

He freely continued his defense.

"And I'm not trained?"

"You're a spy, not an assassin. Infiltrating the Kuklovod requires deft skills of both."

"Well, it's a good thing we're combining forces then."

Lexie stopped and shot him a look.

"Who said anything about combining forces? I said I'm going to retrieve the missiles and you're going to go home. Where did you read into things that we were going together?"

Flynn stopped. No more biting banter. It was time to dig in.

"No, Lexie. I'm coming. You need me as much as I need you."

"Speak for yourself."

Flynn's direct approach wasn't working. He needed leverage on her.

"So, how's your father doing?"

Lexie put her fork down and stopped. Her sudden shift in demeanor from tough gal to despondent woman signaled to Flynn that maybe the old Lexie was still in there somewhere.

"He's doing OK from what I heard last."

"How's his cancer? Still in remission?"

"No, it's come back twice since I saw you last. The doctors say he's only got a few months to live. But you know my dad—he'll fight until the bitter end. He'll probably get twice as long as they say."

"When was the last time you saw him?"

Lexie furrowed her brow and stared at Flynn. "Do you not have any friends in the agency still?"

"Not many—but what's that supposed to mean?"

"It means you haven't heard about me. I'm on a watch list of sorts. There's no way I can go back into the country without getting arrested."

"Seriously?"

"Yeah. Seriously, genius," Lexie said, cutting deep with her sarcasm. "If you haven't figured out that I'm not exactly on the up-and-up any more, your training has almost all been forgotten."

"Well, maybe I can help you out there. Maybe get you in the country to see your father while there's still time."

Lexie started to tear up. She put down her spatula and sought out a tissue. Flynn knew how much she hated showing any kind of feminine emotion, especially water works. It wasn't her style. Yet, here she was, dabbing her eyes and inhaling deep in an effort to fight back what she considered a sign of weakness.

"How could you do that?"

"Well, this mission is more than just rendering the Kuklovod's missile arsenal inoperable. There's something else."

"Oh, what is it?"

"The Kuklovod has Sandford's daughter, Sydney. They're using her to blackmail Sandford into doing their bidding. And they'll kill her if I don't rescue her."

"Why should I care about her?"

"Look, maybe if you come with me and we rescue her, I can pull some strings for you and get you back in the country. I know that Sandford would be willing to overlook whatever offenses the government has against you at this point."

"Wasn't saving your sorry butt last night enough? I could've left you for dead, but I like you too much. Now eat up."

Flynn stared at Lexie. For all her sassiness, he still had a thing for her. His on-again-off-again flings with her in the field grew tiresome, mostly because he wished it would just stay on. Flynn knew at some point he had to move on, so he tried. Not seeing her for a long time made it easier. But here she was, warts and all, standing in front of him just like old times. And those feelings started rushing back.

He smiled as he gobbled down the breakfast. She smiled back.

"Eat up, Flynn. I guess we've now got a big day ahead of us."

Flynn nodded. He thanked her for breakfast and took his plate to the sink once he finished.

Then he collapsed to the floor.

CHAPTER 52

JUST BEFORE SIX O'CLOCK on Sunday morning, Gerald Sandford rumbled down the hall of the third floor at Walter Reed National Military Medical Center in Bethesda, Maryland. Members of the Secret Service nodded to Sandford and his entourage, already alerted to his presence and intention to visit President Briggs. As Sandford passed the final security checkpoint, one of the guards issued a perfunctory wave after acknowledging him with a salute. Sandford's entourage remained there while he neared Briggs' room. But just outside, Sandford met some resistance in the form of Dr. Grant.

"Hello, Mr. Vice President Sandford," Dr. Grant said rather innocuously. But it irritated Sandford.

"Currently, it's President Sandford—and I need to see Arthur Briggs right now."

Dr. Grant glanced down at his chart before pushing his glasses up on his nose. "I'm afraid I can't allow that right now."

"Why not? Is he still in a coma?"

"I can't actually release any information about his status unless the family allows me to. Unfortunately, they haven't. I can tell you that he's resting comfortably and needs to refrain from seeing any visitors."

"We have a national security matter right now and I need to know if he's fit to lead the country. You must at least be able to tell me that."

"Sir, I'm not the one to make that call. He and his family are the ones who determine that."

"Well, if you can't tell me his current medical condition, you can tell me whether you believe he wrote this letter."

Sandford pulled out of his inner coat pocket the letter purportedly from Briggs requesting immediate reinstatement. He handed it to Dr. Grant, who began scanning the letter.

"Look," Dr. Grant said, handing the letter back, "I didn't see him sign this letter, if that's what you mean. But that looks like his signature to me."

"Thanks for your time, Dr. Grant. I won't forget this."

Sandford turned around and huffed away. *I'm going to make sure that doctor gets fired. What is wrong with these people? Why won't anyone give me what I want?*

One way or another, Sandford was going to get what he wanted. He felt like it wasn't too much to ask. What he wanted was simple – a set of launch codes and his daughter back.

Once he returned to his car, his private phone buzzed.

"Have you got good news for me?" Sandford asked.

"Yes. I found you a man."

"Make it happen."

Sandford hung up and smiled. Diane Dixon's little run around didn't matter. He only needed a few more hours to launch his plan—and a flurry of missiles at Russia.

CHAPTER 53

OSBORNE BALANCED A CUP OF COFFEE between his legs as he drove to CIA headquarters. He hadn't heard from Flynn in a while and grew more concerned with each passing minute. *Why hasn't he called me yet?*

It wasn't uncommon for Flynn to skip a check-in or two while on a mission. But this felt different for some reason. Flynn usually didn't go this long without consulting him. It shouldn't have taken him this long to get set up.

Osborne pulled up to the guardhouse in front of the CIA and handed over his credentials.

"Working early today, Mr. Osborne?" the guard asked.

"You know our work is never done."

The guard chuckled. "I know that's right. Too many crazies out there right now. Have a good day, sir."

The guard handed Osborne his credentials and raised the arm on the gate.

While Osborne parked and walked to his desk, he continued to worry about Flynn. He second-guessed his decision to ever send the former operative on such a mission. If truth be told, he knew better. An active, more trained operative would have been more suited to tackle the covert nature of the directive. Yet there wasn't anyone else Osborne trusted more—active or retired. Flynn was his man—he also might be Osborne's undoing at the agency.

Osborne reached his office and shut the door behind him. He took the last swig of his coffee before sitting down and rolling up his sleeves.

His first order of business was to check all possible secure lines of communication. His encrypted voice mail. His secure email. Nothing. Even the most recent terrorist chatter report failed to yield any significant news—or even a hint of what might be happening abroad.

He slumped back in his chair, running his hands through his hair. Frustration mixed with fear resulted in a sick feeling.

Suddenly, his phone buzzed. He lunged for it, hoping to see a familiar number on his screen. It wasn't the number he wanted to see; it was Sandford.

After exchanging pleasantries, Sandford went straight for the point.

"I hope you weren't jerking me around about not having any operatives on active missions in Russia right now."

"Why's that, sir?"

"Because I'm about to light it up. Everything is falling into place for me to launch a volley of missiles into Russia."

"But, sir, you can't do that," Osborne protested.

"I have no choice."

"Please hold off as long as you can. I actually do have someone on the ground who might be able to mitigate the situation."

"What exactly do you mean by that?"

Osborne bit his lip. He carefully selected his words, hoping it wasn't a lie. "I think we can get your daughter back without launching a single missile."

"How are you going to do that?"

"There's a covert mission under way right now. I just need a few more hours to verify the mission's success." Another potential lie. Osborne had backed himself into a corner and knew the only way out was if Flynn came through—an unknown variable at this point.

"I'll give you four hours," Sandford said. "If I don't hear from you by then, I'm going to fire first and ask questions later. Got it?"

"Yes, sir. I got it. I'll call you by 10:30 a.m."

Osborne hung up. As if things weren't bad enough, they now grew worse. Flynn was living ten hours ahead of him, but it did nothing to ease Osborne's angst. In action or not, a clock ticked away—and he had no idea if Flynn was even still alive, much less in position to avert a potential world war in less than four hours.

CHAPTER 54

FLYNN AWOKE TO A SEARING sore neck. It didn't take him long to realize why when he went to rub it. The handcuffs chaining him to the iron bedpost over Lexie's bed ensured that wouldn't happen without much effort. He looked at the clock. It was five-thirty in the evening and the sun was already dipping below the Urals in Khanty-Mansiysk. No sign of Lexie.

Flynn let out a scream of frustration, angered over trusting someone he knew he shouldn't have. Lexie's intoxicating charm burned him several times when they worked together—but nothing like this. It was as if Lexie has fully embraced her darker side. *She doesn't even care to see her dying father. Pathetic.* He rattled the handcuffs again but to no avail. It only made him feel more foolish.

Sulking and yelling let out the steam Flynn needed to release—but it did nothing to change his current situation. He surveyed the structure of the bedposts, looking for any way to get free or move.

Near the top of each iron post, Flynn noticed a decorative ball. *I hope this isn't just a decoration.* Flynn twisted his body so his feet could reach the ball. Clamping his feet around the ball, he began to slowly turn the ball, loosening it. After about three minutes of careful foot-work, the ball bounced onto the wooden floor, freeing the ironwork that served as the headboard from the post. He flipped his body in the other direction and began working the counterpart ball off the post. Once it hit the ground, he jammed the ironwork toward the wall as it disengaged from the bedpost completely. He wasn't exactly free, but walking around attached to a bedpost was far better than being immobile and fastened to one.

Flynn maneuvered awkwardly around the room, searching for something to jimmy the lock. That's when he spotted the key to the cuffs on the kitchen counter. Flynn smiled at Lexie's arrogance—for once he appreciated it. He grabbed the key with his mouth and sat down on the floor in the living room. Employing his feet again, Flynn grabbed the key with his toes and inserted it into one of the cuffs. Using both his feet, he carefully turned the key until one of the cuffs released. He then used his hand to unlock the other one and free himself.

Osborne!

Flynn had nearly forgotten he promised Osborne a call. He needed to at least let his handler know he was still alive and that there were new complications in completing the mission.

He fished out his phone and called Osborne. *Come on, pick up!*

After Osborne answered, Flynn wasted no time.

"It's me, Flynn. How's everything going?"

"Not good. What about with you? I've been worried since I hadn't heard from you in a while. I thought maybe the Russians got to you."

"Not a chance. But things here are complicated."

"How come?"

"Lexie Martin."

"What the heck is she doing there?"

"It's a long story and I don't have time to get into it. But she's here and she's after the missiles too—but for entirely different motives."

"Look, you can't let her run off with the missiles—and you don't have much time."

Flynn brushed off Osborne's sense of urgency. With Osborne, everything was always on the brink of disaster.

"I know, I know. I should be able to make contact with some of our assets here and neutralize the Kuklovod tomorrow."

"No, Flynn. You're not listening to me. You don't have much time. In three hours if Sandford doesn't hear from me that you've secured the weapons and rescued his daughter, he's going to send a volley of missiles into Russia. We're only hours away from starting an unnecessary crisis, if not worse."

"Three hours! Are you out of your mind?" Flynn could hardly wrap his mind around how he might be able to pull off the mission in such a short amount of time.

"No, I'm not out of my mind, but Sandford is. They're threatening to kill Sydney still if he doesn't launch the missiles within a short time frame—and he's decided to acquiesce to their demands."

"Can't Briggs' stop him?"

"Apparently not. Some of his cabinet members are trying to revoke Sandford's power, but those efforts have failed so far. It's up to you at this point. So, if I don't hear from you in the next three hours, you just might be stuck in Russia. Just pray where you are isn't a target."

"OK, I'll think of something." Flynn wondered why he had ever agreed to this fool's errand, which now looked more like a death sentence.

"Just call me as soon as you know something. I'm counting on you."

"That makes one of us."

"Good luck, Flynn."

Flynn hung up and let out another scream. The odds for completing this mission had just moved from unlikely to impossible. But it wasn't going to stop him from trying.

CHAPTER 55

GERALD SANDFORD PACED IN HIS OFFICE. He managed to bully his way into position to cave to the Kuklovod's request—but at what cost? His rogue actions would indeed cost him every ounce of power he sacrificed to obtain. But he considered it worth it. Anything just to see his sweet Sydney's face again.

His phone rang and it was Diane Dixon.

"I think we need to talk," she said.

"About what?"

"You know what—restoring the presidency to its rightful owner."

"Diane, there's nothing more I would rather do than give the office back to Arthur, but he can't lead. He's still in a coma."

"And who told you that?"

"I saw him myself at Walter Reed."

"That's hardly possible since he's up and moving about. Gerald, you've always been a terrible liar."

"I'm not lying. I'm calling your bluff. I know what you're trying to do—and so help me God once this is over with, I'm going to destroy you."

"Don't you threaten me, Gerald. You might have everyone else believing your story—but I know the truth. I know you never saw him. You won't either. In fact, I doubt you'll ever see your office again after today. I know what you did at Strategic Command, and I plan to let the American people know about it too. You don't have to do this."

"You have no idea what I have to do or why I have to do it. But

214 | R.J. PATTERSON

your threats bear no weight on me. I'm doing this for the good of the country."

"Stop lying to yourself. You're doing this to avenge Sydney's death—plain and simple. You're a bitter man and you're doing to die that way, disgraced as you leave public office. I'm going to make sure of that."

"You do what you've got to do, Diane. Just know there's always a price for such actions. I'm sure your sixteen-year-old daughter would love to find out tomorrow on national television that her father is actually Arthur Briggs. Talk about your scandals."

Diane went silent, so much so that Sandford wondered if she hung up.

"Diane? Diane? You still there?"

"Yes," she mumbled.

"Good. I just want to you to understand that when you force my hand, you're not going to like what you see. There's more of your dirty little laundry I wouldn't mind airing if necessary. So, just quit passing around that forged little document and keep quiet while I do what Arthur Briggs can't right now—lead a nation."

He hung up, hoping never to hear from Diane again. She always rubbed him the wrong way, especially after Arthur told him their dirty little secret one night after having a few too many glasses of Scotch. Sandford never mentioned it again—until now. He knew it was the kind of information that would one day serve a useful purpose.

It was eight-thirty and still no call from Osborne.

Sandford took another call from his new general at Strategic Command with a list of all the target sites. Twelve missiles in all were set to launch toward Russia, inflicting severe damage if they all hit their targets. The casualties would be in the hundreds of thousands, according to early prognostications.

Sandford looked over the list: Moscow, St. Petersburg, Perm, Novosibirsk, Omsk, Kazan, Tyumen, Khanty-Mansiysk. Just a bunch of names of cities.

He authorized the list and faxed it back to Strategic Command.

CHAPTER 56

FLYNN GATHERED HIS GEAR and headed out the door. If Lexie intended to taunt him by leaving his gear around so he could see it while chained to her bed, she failed. But he felt as if failure might be imminent for his own mission. Three hours to infiltrate the Kuklovod's base camp and secure the missiles? He placed the odds of succeeding just below achieving world peace.

But odds meant there was always a chance—and this was a chance worth taking.

Flynn took a taxi to one of the more popular trailheads just north of town that ran along the Ob River. He estimated it was at least an hour's hike across the rugged terrain of the ascending Urals to reach the secluded base camp. Less than a hundred yards after walking down the marked trail, Flynn veered off into a heavily wooded area. Relying on CIA satellite imaging topography maps, he marched toward his destination. The sun edged down toward the nearest mountain's apex for the evening and then slipped behind it. The natural light wouldn't last much longer.

Through the woods he trudged, splitting his time between thinking about his plan and retracing the steps that led him here. Execution was simple if all of Osborne's intel proved accurate. But he knew better than to count on that. Such folly led to the early demise of many naïve agents. *You know what you know.* It was a mantra he developed a long time ago while on a mission in Angola. He was tasked with meeting an informant in a rural farming area. The informant reportedly knew all the details about a terrorist camp the CIA noticed on satellite surveillance. To Flynn, nothing seemed difficult about the assignment. Pose as an aide worker with an organization doing regular work there, deliver some seeds to a local farmer, get the information, go home. Simple. Yet it proved to be anything but that.

Once Flynn dropped off the seeds, three armed guards ambushed him. Nothing beforehand had suggested any potential problems. But it was a disaster. Two aide workers got shot before Flynn mitigated the situation by immobilizing two of the attackers and shooting the other in the head. Fortunately, the situation proved to be invaluable as he gained more intel on the camp than he would've ever received from the farmer. Less than two hours of torture techniques and Flynn learned all he needed to know from the captive terrorists. He even released them to warn the camp of an impending strike, but it was a wasted effort. A drone strike annihilated the camp less than five minutes after Flynn called it in.

You know what you know—and then you find out some more. All Flynn knew at this point was that he had to immobilize a half-dozen guards before reaching the Kuklovod's command center and taking it off-line. What he didn't know was how Lexie would figure into the equation. Would she muddle his plan? Turn on him? Prove to be an ally? Nothing was for certain at this point. So he stuck to the plan. *You know what you know.*

He slogged through a slew of tributaries snaking off from the Ob River with only the dusky sky to light his way. Flynn turned on his lantern and proceeded forward. It wasn't long before he reached a clearing and identified the scattered lights as the Kuklovod's compound. He switched off his lantern and moved cautiously toward the guarded facility, using the tree line as a shield.

Flynn checked his watch. Only two hours remained until his deadline to inform Osborne of his successful mission—if was indeed successful. Despite the time crunch, Flynn refused to botch the mission by trying to play cowboy. His own life depended on his ability to correctly assess the situation before charging in—and this wasn't an easy task. For the next ten minutes, he observed the repetitive movements of the guards. They all smoked, as if it was the only way to survive the monotony of protecting the perimeter of a building nestled deep in the Urals. It was surely an uneventful assignment. But not tonight.

In an effort to penetrate the building as stealthily as possible, Flynn chose to use his knife. He tossed a rock in the woods to turn the guard's attention in the opposite direction before sneaking up behind him and slitting his throat. He dragged his body into the woods and rolled it behind a log. But not before he stole the guard's earpiece so he could pick up the impending chatter that would explode if his presence was realized.

Flynn eliminated the second guard moments later by slipping up behind him and snatching his cigarette. When the confused guard turned around, Flynn stabbed him in the throat while covering the man's mouth. He moved this guard's body into the woods as well before approaching his most difficult target—the guard tower.

Hidden in the shadows of the tree line, Flynn watched the rhythms of the guard tower's spotlight. At first glance, it appeared to move haphazardly, but it didn't take Flynn long to see that the chaotic pattern was nothing close to chaotic. It moved systematically across the compound perimeter—and Flynn recognized his opportunity to strike.

Quietly climbing the tower, Flynn timed his lurch perfectly. He lunged off the top step with his knife and landed it into the back of the oblivious guard. The pattern took a short hiatus before Flynn took control of the spotlight and kept the rhythm going. Nobody on the inside suspected a thing, as no squawking blared from his radio. All was quiet, but not for long.

Flynn leapt over the guard tower and scurried down the inside of the perimeter fence. He went to the door his intel told him was the most lax when it came to guard presence. Using the security decryption device Osborne gave him, Flynn attached it to the keypad and waited while it found the right combination to gain entry. It didn't take long before Flynn was in the building.

He crept down the dimly lit hall. It was empty. Not a soul in sight. He waited for a few seconds to see if he could detect any noise at all, any potential presence of guards. Nothing. And nothing on the radio either.

This is going to be easier than I thought. Flynn turned the corner and jumped back. He saw a guard sitting outside an unidentified room. Then Flynn poked his head around the corner again only to realize the guard was asleep. He ripped open his pack and pulled out a handkerchief and some chloroform. He slipped up to the guard and shoved it forcefully under his nose. The man barely flinched, remaining in his dozed position—head down, feet stretched out in front of him.

Flynn peered inside the door but didn't see his target. He continued down the hall a few more feet before he heard a familiar voice.

"Where do you think you're going?"

Flynn spun around. Pointing a gun at him from twenty feet away was Ivan.

CHAPTER 57

NINETY MINUTES. COME ON, FLYNN. Give me a call.

Osborne stared at the phone on his desk. It didn't blink or buzz or ring. He wanted to rip it out of the wall and scream. Just destroy something, anything. The waiting was killing him. It wasn't like he had never been through something like this before with Flynn.

During a reconnaissance mission to Malaysia, Flynn got made by a Chinese spy who was selling U.S. government secrets. The directive was simple: find out who was buying the secrets. But Flynn wasn't careful enough. Two members of the Chinese spy's security detail apprehended Flynn and held him for the duration of the supposed time of the transaction. They blindfolded him and threw him in a holding cell near the location of the meet. For three days, Osborne waited. Not a word from Flynn. Osborne feared his best operative died somehow. Three days was an eternity in the world of espionage. Plans could be hatched, divulged, set into motion and squashed during that time. Yet, nothing from Flynn.

Finally, Flynn had called Osborne, letting him know that he was all right. His mission was a failure—sort of. He didn't get the information he came for, but the Chinese spy and his associates were all murdered. The buyer only performed a cursory search of the building, which gave Flynn the break he needed to remain hidden. He eventually worked himself free and escaped to view the carnage.

Osborne knew it was far too early to give up on Flynn now, but this situation was different. He could spend time handwringing over the possible death of a mission agent—and it was justified, yet part of the job.

Presiding over a mission that could determine the fate of millions and set into motion a world war was beyond Osborne's scope of familiarity. This new territory set him on edge. An acting president hell-bent on blowing up half of Russia. An extremist group determined to start a world war. And a former operative on his first mission in years to keep it all from happening. It was a recipe for angst on the highest level.

Osborne's phone rang. It was Sandford.

"Where are we at? I've got missiles being loaded as we speak."

"Nothing yet, sir. But we've still got ninety more minutes. Please be patient." Osborne was telling Sandford that as much as he was telling himself.

"We've been far too patient with these people. It's time to take action."

"Just hold off, please, sir."

"Ninety minutes—then we're firing the missiles."

Sandford hung up.

Osborne stared at the clock. He only had eighty-nine minutes now.

CHAPTER 58

FLYNN LAID DOWN his Glock 26 and stared at the familiar figure aiming a gun at him down the dimly lit hallway. Less than forty-eight hours ago, the two men fought in Flynn's home—and Flynn let him live. Now they stood on Ivan's turf, half a world away. Flynn determined he wouldn't make the same mistake twice.

"Существует кто-то, кто хочет тебя видеть," Ivan said in Russian.

Someone wants to see me. This should be interesting. Flynn moved slowly toward Ivan, hands raised in a surrendered position. By the time Flynn reached Ivan, two guards joined them and quickly patted down Flynn. Satisfied that he was weaponless, they ushered him down a long dark hallway and through a bevy of rooms. Unfinished concrete floors and cinder block walls formed the structure for the facility's maze-like layout. Flynn tried to ascertain where he was in the building based on the blueprints the CIA gave him. The better bearings he possessed, the better chance he could escape alive—if ever given the chance.

What the building lacked in aesthetics, it made up for with its state-of-the-art security system. Each room required a retinal scan for entry as well as an alternating code displayed on a digital fob carried by each guard. Flynn noticed a digital clock on the wall. The bright red numbers reminded him he had barely an hour to secure the facility and call Osborne. Ushered deeper into the recesses of the building in silence, Flynn wondered if perhaps the blueprints were faulty or from an early phase of construction.

After nearly five minutes, they arrived at their destination: the control room for the facility's missile silo.

Fluorescent lights flickered and hummed in one vacant corner of the room. At the far end of the room, a team of four men pushed glowing buttons and flicked switches, calling out commands in Russian. Flynn watched as the men wheeled across the stark white floor and ran through a checklist to apparently prepare a missile launch. He understood from their chatter that a launch was scheduled to occur in sixty minutes.

"Принеси мне девушки," Ivan announced as they entered the room.

Flynn froze and stared as the man sitting in the largest chair spun around. Wearing a long dark trench coat, the man stood up and walked toward Flynn. His dark skin bunched in wrinkles around his forehead and extended onto his baldhead. Using a black wooden cane, the man shuffled toward Flynn. His small brown eyes directed a piercing stare at his visitor. Once he arrived within three feet of Flynn, he stopped.

"Mr. Flynn," the man said, speaking in a thick Russian accent. "It is a pleasure to finally meet you here on our terms. For your sake, I wish it could have been under different conditions, for this will not end well for you. You had your chance to ensure that it did, but you continued to meddle where you didn't belong."

Flynn furrowed his brow and stared at the man, wondering if he was supposed to know him.

"What's the matter, Mr. Flynn? Do you not recognize me? Perhaps you might know who I was if I still had all my hair. But I lost that a long time ago—along with all my faith in humanity."

"The red-haired negro," Flynn muttered to himself. But it was loud enough that the man heard him.

"That's probably my favorite alias, though a more formal introduction is required in this instance. My name is Marcos Buscape."

Flynn stared, unaware that the name should mean anything. It certainly wasn't a name he ever heard while working at the agency.

The man continued.

"I understand if you've never heard of me—most people haven't. And quite frankly, I prefer to keep it that way. The less people of your ilk know about me, the better. I don't even like it when our committed organization here gets mentioned in the press. We like to work behind the scenes. Our work isn't about glory—it's about an end game that will better this world, far more than I can say for your American imperialism."

Flynn wanted to lash out at the man, dispute his claims. But he chose not to. The more his enemy talked, the more he would know how to defeat him.

"But you ruined all that for us when you went on television and alerted the world to our presence. The Kuklovod is a long-standing order that seeks to influence people and world events, not grandstand. Yet we can't do anything now without people seeing us as an evil group. If your President Bush were still blathering on about terrorism, we'd be part of his axis of evil, I'm sure."

Flynn, who bit his tongue while scanning the room, couldn't resist the urge to stay silent any longer. He had a few questions of his own and needed to do some probing.

"So, now you're just going to start a world war?" Flynn asked.

"Oh, we aren't starting anything—we're merely ensuring that it happens. For far too long, Russia and the United States have played nice, acting like two comrades instead of mortal enemies. Both countries have lacked the leadership with the fortitude to attack the other. And we didn't mind since we have no interest in seeing your failed imperialistic ideas spread here and beyond. But as your weak-kneed government has dwindled its military, Russia has been advancing its technology and strengthening its army in ways you never dreamed possible. Now with the upper hand, Russia only needs an excuse to strike. Unlike you Americans, Russia would never strike first in an unprovoked act. But get the right American leader in power—and everything goes boom!"

Buscape stamped his cane on the floor for emphasis. He then leaked a wry smile, apparently proud of the plan he conceived to stoke the embers of war.

Seeking a deeper grasp of his enemy, Flynn went fishing with his next statement.

"You certainly don't look like a Russian," Flynn said.

Buscape glared at Flynn a moment before speaking.

"That is the problem with you Americans—it's always about appearances. How one looks determines a person's value. Are they beautiful? Successful? Rich? Powerful? And look where it's gotten you—a depraved country lacking in discipline, leadership and compassion. The land of opportunity is now a cesspool of narcissism. If you think I'm doing this because I have ties to Russia, you are wrong. My passion is to see the world consumed by true communism—where we share what we have, despising those who clamor over others to get their way. It's about seeing a collective good emerge from a world currently devoid of compassion."

"So you kill millions of innocent people to achieve this brand of communism, forcing them into this ideal?"

Buscape looked at the floor, dragging his cane around in circles as he thought. He finally looked up at Flynn.

"Yes," he said, nodding his head. "If I must, I will. Their lives are meaningless now anyway. Better that they die sooner than later to save them from a vacant existence. The result will be a better world—the kind of world my father dreamed of."

"Your father?"

"Yes, my father—a real father. Father Buscape. You've likely never heard of him as he toiled away in Luanda, Angola, wasting away in the final years of his life without ever seeing his dream realized. He offered me up as a sacrifice to Ilya Makarova, the founder of the Kuklovod. In exchange for my service to Ilya, my father would receive all the funding he needed to help establish a Communist party in Angola. My father may have failed to see true communism spread like he hoped, but I won't. Today will mark the dawn of a new day in the earth's history."

Flynn grew tired of the old man spouting his misguided idealism. Despite all of the awful things Flynn had to do in the name of protecting the freedom of the American people, he knew people don't change by force. Strangely enough, he shared some of Buscape's sentiments, but starting a war was no way to accomplish it—nor would it ever accomplish anything in the end other than more war. He wasn't about to let the codger take millions of innocent lives.

With two guards watching Flynn's every twitch, he needed a distraction. Flynn bent over and started coughing, catching the guards by surprise as they knelt down next to him to see what was wrong. Flynn then wrapped his leg around the neck of the guard on his left, forcing him to drop his assault weapon. At the same time, he kicked the knee of the guard on his right, sending him to the floor. Flynn snatched the weapon off the floor and jammed it up against Buscape's neck, careful not to cut him.

Ivan, who had holstered his weapon, redrew but not soon enough. A standoff began.

"Everybody drop your weapons … now!" Flynn directed as he maneuvered behind Buscape to utilize him as a shield. "The rest of you, up against the wall!"

The three men remaining at the control panel joined Ivan and the two guards, standing with their backs to the wall.

Ivan refused to budge.

"I said drop your weapons!" Flynn yelled again.

Ivan held fast.

Then Buscape spoke. "It's OK, son. You can put down your weapon. He's not going to harm you—or me either."

Flynn waited until Ivan dropped his gun before responding.

"Listen, Buscape. I already made that mistake once. I'm not leaving Ivan alive this time."

Buscape then began chuckling to himself, nearly uncontrollably.

"You Americans never cease to amaze me with you brash arrogance."

Flynn pressed the tip of the rifle deeper into Buscape's neck.

"Принеси мне девушки!" Buscape yelled.

A side door swung open and Lexie marched out, gagged with her hands tied behind her back. Even more surprising was the person holding a gun to Lexie's head.

It was Sydney Sandford.

CHAPTER 59

GERALD SANDFORD READ the text message on his phone. He brushed back a tear that streaked down his face. Seeing Sydney bound enraged him. Her face appeared bruised, her body beaten. If Sandford could stand in front of her kidnappers at the moment, he was certain he would beat them to death.

But he couldn't. All he could do was meet the demands of her captors. So what if it started a war? What kind of father wouldn't move heaven and earth for his daughter?

Thirty minutes was all he had left to comply with their demands. Still no word from Osborne.

Seconds dripped by like hours, each one stirring up an ocean of emotions within him. He remembered saying good-bye to Sydney as she embarked on her Peace Corps mission to Russia. No matter how much he tried to protect her, Sandford never could sway her to follow in his footsteps. She wanted to change the world and make a difference in the lives of others. He pleaded with her to pursue that noble mission through politics and embrace the path he blazed for her. And Sydney almost went for it.

When she was nineteen, Sydney took off a year from school to help with her father's U.S. Senate re-election campaign. The brutal spring primary set Sandford up for a bare-knuckle brawl in the November general election. Heading into the final two weeks before the election, Sandford trailed by eight points in the polls. The poor polling numbers prompted some major donors to decline to contribute further when Sandford

228 | R.J. PATTERSON

needed it most. He even watched several key campaign staff members exit early, fearing the worst.

But if voters hadn't voted, Sandford assumed there was always ample time to change their minds.

Three days before the election, a scandal broke: Pictures emerged of Jim Dyer in suggestive situations with a prostitute. Making the scandal worse was Dyer's platform plank of family values. His wife and three children stood by him as he railed against "dirty politics," denying the incident ever occurred.

The last polling numbers the day before the election showed a swing of fifteen points, giving Sandford an advantage of seven percentage points. Sandford won by twenty percent.

At the celebration party, Sydney began talking with one of her father's staff members, whose loose lips let out the campaign's secret: the Dyer incident was set up. Sandford's staff hired a prostitute to seduce Dyer months earlier but failed. So, this time they left nothing to chance, drugging Dyer and staging the photos. Nothing even happened. But the photos suggested otherwise.

Sydney took the information to her father, who denied any knowledge of it. She begged him to apologize and tell the truth, but he refused. "It's just politics," he told her. "It was for the good of the people anyway. He only cares about power, not about helping the people."

That was when Sandford started to lose his daughter—and when she lost faith in using politics as a way to transform the world. A few years later, she was heading off to Russia to help people there. Sandford never dreamed that would be the last time he saw her again. Yet after thinking she was dead for years, he would do anything to touch her again, to hold his little girl and say he was sorry for all that he'd done. He'd be a different man, a better father.

But none of it would happen until he launched a full-scale missile attack on Russia.

CHAPTER 60

FLYNN STARED AT LEXIE as she struggled under Sydney's tight grip. Reading the situation wasn't easy. Lexie faced the men Flynn had ordered to line up against the wall. If she tried to signal anything, they just might tip off Sydney. It was up to Flynn to send her a message that would help him squash the sudden quagmire.

"Sydney—so nice of you to join us," Buscape said, turning to face her as Flynn continued to press the tip of his barrel into the old man's neck. "I think this is what we call a stand off."

Flynn tried to hide his emotions. He considered the possibility of acting like he didn't care about Lexie. And on some level, he didn't. It was her arrogance that led to this predicament. Yet he needed her. This mission would fail if he didn't have some help. Despite his urge to blow her off, he couldn't let Sydney—or anyone else from the Kuklovod— kill Lexie. At this point, he didn't even care if she made off with the missiles; he just wanted to stop a war from igniting.

Glancing behind him, Flynn noticed Ivan and the operators hadn't moved. Buscape hardly struggled as he was too weak to overpower Flynn and seemed keenly aware of that fact. But in front of Flynn stood his biggest challenge: Sydney holding Lexie hostage.

Running out of time, Flynn needed to devise a plan quickly. *Maybe I can reason with her?*

"Sydney, I know your father is worried sick about you," Flynn began. "Why don't you put the gun down so you can go home and pre-vent the loss of innocent life?"

Sydney laughed. "You think that CIA voodoo is going to work on me? I already know what's in your playbook and I've got a plan for everything. So, if you want to try some of your pop psychology on me, be my guest. But if you knew me well enough, you'd know that trying to use my father to connect with me is a big mistake."

Flynn knew it was a mistake the second he started speaking aloud. But it bought him more time to consider a way out.

"Sydney, what happened to you?" Flynn asked. "You were so idealistic and driven—now you seem jaded, angry … distant."

"Do you want me to lay on a couch or something? Let me tell you all my deepest desires? Is this how you think this is going to go?" Sydney asked. Her biting sarcasm contradicted the pleasant demeanor that Osborne said she had. Apparently, charm had since escaped her command.

With the Kuklovod tattoo emblazoned on the corner of her neck, Sydney exhibited the opposite of every trait Osborne had attributed to her.

Though Sydney was beautiful, Flynn had to look hard to see it. The high cheekbones and curvaceous figure remained mostly hidden by a tough exterior Sydney worked tirelessly to promote. The idealistic girl that once inhabited her body wasn't gone and buried yet. Sydney exuded plenty of idealism, but it was muddied by her newfound communist philosophy.

Flynn thought hard. He needed a signal for Lexie.

"No, Sydney, that's not how this is going to go," Flynn said. "I thought it might go something like it went in Cameroon."

Before Sydney could respond to Flynn's cryptic answer, Lexie swung into action. She spun hard to her left, exposing Sydney's back to Flynn. He released Buscape for a moment, only to fire off a short burst toward Sydney, striking her in the left shoulder. It was enough to incapacitate her for a few minutes and give Lexie the chance to help him gain the upper hand.

Lexie snatched a knife off Sydney, and she was able to cut herself free. After that, she grabbed Sydney's gun. Meanwhile, Sydney screamed out in agony as she writhed around on the floor now coated in her blood.

"Let's tie them up," Flynn said.

"Go for it," Lexie answered, tossing him a handful of rope and duct tape she found laying on a desk at the far end of the room. "I'll give you some cover."

Flynn tied up each man as quickly as possible. The time sped by but he secured Buscape, Ivan, and the remaining men within five minutes. He then turned his attention to Sydney.

Sydney lay still on the floor. He wasn't even sure she was still alive until he checked for her pulse and found it. Maybe it was shock or trauma from the loss of blood—but she was out. Nevertheless, Flynn wasn't taking any chances. He wound the duct tape tight around her wrists, securing her arms behind her back then her feet as well.

Flynn checked the clock. Twenty minutes.

"Let's move, Lexie. We don't have much time."

As Flynn stood up, he looked at his former partner. No longer was the gun trained on their fellow hostages. Lexie was pointing her gun at Flynn.

CHAPTER 61

DIANE DIXON SAT in the private waiting room with Bethany Briggs. The First Lady did her best to hold it together in public, but now she was away from the watchful eyes of reporters and television cameras. Alone with her thoughts and a trusted friend, Bethany's tears flowed freely.

Diane watched as Bethany buried her head in her hands and heaved sobs of deep grief. It pained her to watch a woman so sophisticated become unraveled, no matter how justifiable it was. She reached out to hold Bethany's hand. It was clammy and cold, nothing like the warm touch Bethany usually exuded when she welcomed someone politely with her stately handshake.

Standing by her husband through years of diplomacy, Bethany understood how a politician's wife should act—and she played her part well. Always looking flawless for the cameras, smiling and waving, performing an inordinate amount of charity work. Diane admired that about her, though at the same time pitied her for the role. With Bethany's diplomatic skills and compassionate wisdom, Diane believed Bethany was better suited for the Oval Office than her husband. And whenever some wonderfully crafted idea emerged from the President's desk, Diane suspected it originated elsewhere.

But now, Diane watched Bethany turned into a heap of bitter tears. While her husband may have lacked the guts the hawks in America demanded, Arthur Briggs was beloved by most. President Briggs believed the nation needed healing from a string of presidencies bent on dividing a torn country. His selection of Gerald Sandford as his running mate proved how it was possible to work politically with someone who shared far different values and ideas. Compromise was a touchstone of Briggs' presidency—and the American people prospered because of it.

When the war drums began to thump, Briggs' strength became his weakness. The unified front splintered, forming various factions that stood both for and against the war on many varying levels. Some groups wanted to send nuclear bombs into Russia. Others wanted to simply send a message. While still others insisted that there was no cause for concern and America should ignore the missile silos being erected in Siberia. The peace crowd saw it as typical Russian grandstanding rather than a saber-rattling move. In the end, Briggs was left with a mess, one that looked like someone fired a missile into his staff. While he lay unconscious in the hospital, Briggs never would have guessed his cabinet would take divisiveness in American politics to another level. Nor would he have ever guessed that Sandford would ignore his wishes and angle to strike first against Russia.

Diane watched Bethany's anguish as her sobs turned to wails.

"Why Arthur?" Bethany cried. "He's such a good man!"

Diane withdrew for a moment, uncomfortable at the outburst of raw emotion. She let Bethany simmer for a few moments before speaking.

"I don't know what to say, Bethany," Diane said, clutching her friend's hand again.

Bethany closed her eyes and shook her head. She didn't say a word, but the message was conveyed: Diane didn't need to say anything.

The blurry-eyed women sat motionless for several minutes, save the streaks of mascara oozing down their faces. Briggs wasn't dead yet, but to Diane it felt like the death of his dream for his beloved country.

Suddenly, Dr. Grant burst into the room.

"Mrs. Briggs, Mrs. Briggs, come quick!" he said, motioning to Bethany to join him. "Your husband is awake!"

CHAPTER 62

FLYNN GAZED AT THE MESS next to him on the cold floor. Sydney Sandford's wound continued to ooze large amounts of blood and showed no signs of stopping. He estimated that she would bleed out within the next two minutes if she didn't get some type of medical attention. Though he wasn't on an officially sanctioned CIA mission, he realized it was a near epic fail. Losing the Kuklovod's missiles and gunning down the Vice President's daughter made him look like the agency's most inept operative of all time. Yet there was still time to change all that and avoid CIA infamy. It just wouldn't be easy.

His first issue was escaping the zip ties Lexie used on his hands and feet. In her haste, she neglected to anchor him to a large object. Flynn knocked the bottom heel of his boot three times in succession to release his emergency knife. It was his new favorite feature of all the equipment Osborne had given him. He grabbed it and quickly sawed through the ties on his feet. Then he did the same with his hands.

With his pack strewn in one corner of the room, Flynn grabbed a first aid kit and got to work on Sydney. He began applying pressure to the wound after he poured a disinfectant over it. Within a half a minute, Flynn finished bandaging her up and headed after Lexie.

Then he turned back to Sydney.

"I'm really sorry about all this—you'll be fine," he said.

Flynn's momentary compassion vanished. He needed the same thing Lexie needed to gain access to the missiles—an eye and a corresponding security card. Flynn suspected Ivan's would suffice.

The process was almost as painful for Flynn as it was for his nemesis. Detaching the eyeball of a living person made Flynn feel like a monster— but it would pale in comparison to knowing he could've stopped millions of people from dying yet didn't have the stomach to perform a simple extraction. At first Ivan writhed in pain, showering Flynn with his vicious hate. Unmoved, Flynn decided the more humane thing would be to incapacitate him first—so he shoved a handkerchief loaded with chloroform onto Ivan's mouth before he began to root out Ivan's eye. It didn't take long. Flynn snatched Ivan's access card and began his pursuit of Lexie.

Flynn raced through two doors before finding the cache of Intercontinental Ballistic Missiles in a large holding facility, just as the blueprints had revealed. As he opened the door, he heard Lexie's feet scuffling across the floor. Then, the door clicked behind him, giving away the element of surprise. The shuffling noise stopped.

Concrete walls held the missiles in a staging area. A mechanized loading system lifted the missiles into the silos for launch. It was in the process of securing one of the missiles into a launch position before it stopped. Aside from the five remaining missiles in the corner of the room, the rest of the space was filled with hydraulic lifts and small construction vehicles. Plenty of hiding places made securing the facility Flynn's nightmare at the moment.

He crept along the outer wall, listening for the slightest sound to give him an indication of where Lexie was. Suddenly the whir of a hydraulic lift echoed throughout the room, masking any footsteps. Instead of letting Lexie use the noise to her advantage alone, he decided to use it to his as he darted toward one of the construction vehicles. Behind him were the missiles.

While Lexie managed to maneuver about the room using a series of distractions, Flynn went to work. He took advantage of each sound to open the missiles' guidance systems and strip them out. He also added a small tracking chip inside each one before putting them back together again. For the next five minutes, he worked fast, dividing his attention between disabling the missiles and avoiding Lexie.

Only one more missile to go.

The final missile sat out in the open. He needed to distract Lexie from what he was doing.

"I thought we were on the same side, Lexie," Flynn said, lifting his head back and speaking straight toward the ceiling. He needed to make his position difficult for her to ascertain.

Lexie said nothing.

While Flynn continued to talk, he also worked at disabling the final missile's guidance system.

"We make a great pair, me and you. Tracking down terrorists and bringing them to justice. What happened to you? When did you lose your way?"

Still nothing. But Flynn didn't care. He was almost finished.

"I even thought your humanity was intact when I asked you about your dad—but apparently that was just one of your ploys to get me to calm down. You never intended to do this with me, did you?"

He reattached the guidance system door and dashed across the room to a position better suited for a shootout, if that was where this confrontation was headed.

Flynn felt the tip of a knife dig into his skin ever so slightly. He raised his hands in surrender.

"No, I never did, Flynn," Lexie said in his ear. "I only saved you so I could gain access to the CIA server and find out what they know about me. But when I learned that you didn't have any way to help me do that, you were of no use to me. Just dead weight, like always."

Flynn tried to ignore the insults.

"I never trusted you, Lexie—but at least you know you can trust me. After all, I did save your life."

"I would've been just fine without you!" she shot back.

"Oh, really? Fine watching your missiles launched into the air after the Vice President's daughter subdued you? I doubt your employers would've been fine with that."

"I only care about results—and a team will be here any moment now to take away these missiles. And there's nothing you're going to be able to do about it. You just better be grateful I'm feeling gracious today, as I'm letting you live."

She reached in his pocket and snatched Ivan's eyeball, throwing it onto the ground and stomping on it. The sight made Flynn flinch. She pushed him toward the door and shoved him inside along with a handgun.

"Good luck!" she yelled and pulled the door shut.

Flynn stared at the room through a large plate-glass window. A door to the outside lowered into the ground, allowing two large semi-trucks to back into the room. Helpless to stop it, Flynn glanced at a clock in the upper corner of the room.

Five minutes! I've gotta call Osborne!

***

GERALD SANDFORD CHECKED HIS WATCH and picked up his phone. The time for waiting was over. It was time for action.

He called Strategic Command and gave the order to prepare for the missile launch. It was time to meet the demands of these terrorists and get his daughter back.

CHAPTER 63

FLYNN LOOKED AT THE LOCKED DOOR feeling helpless. The last remaining piece to complete his mission now lay two rooms away—and he had no way of getting into it. He glanced back out the bay window to watch armed guards loading the missiles onto the trucks. To come so far and so close only to be derailed at this point burned Flynn.

Just think, Flynn. You can do this.

The room was about fifteen feet square and had only an access panel to the connecting rooms and a large window. No furniture, no control panel, no computer system. Just stark concrete gray, top to bottom.

Standing in the middle of the room, he nearly fell to the ground when the entire building was jolted. The men in the holding area all froze too, looking around to see if there might have been an explosion. Flynn moved against the wall closest to the door that led to the control room—and he waited.

Seconds later, two guards burst into the room. They didn't even see Flynn. While they were busy scanning their eyes to gain access to the holding room, Flynn slipped through the open door and into the next room.

Only one more room to go. Just wait.

He checked his watch. Two minutes remained until his deadline to call Osborne.

The seconds trickled by like days as he waited for another break. He couldn't count on it, but it was his only option at this point. Fortunately, two more guards delivered, blasting through the room, oblivious to his presence as he hid crouched in the corner. Flynn darted through the door and into the control room—and the room was ablaze.

Suddenly, all the doors flung open as the fire alarms wailed. The small explosion—whatever it was that caused it—ignited a fire in the control room that led to screams and moans of the guards rendered immobile by Lexie. Flynn scanned the room for his bag and found it, diving into his pack and digging for his phone.

Out of the corner of his eye, he looked up and saw a monstrous sight—Ivan brooding over him, his eye patched. Flynn assumed he somehow got into a first aid pack and saved himself, though he swore Ivan wouldn't have survived based on the amount of blood pooled on the floor, much less been awake at this point. Flynn began dialing the numbers while he fumbled for his gun that he had laid down when he started searching for his phone. Flynn looked up. Ivan was gone.

Flynn stumbled into the hall, dragging his pack behind him. The phone began ringing. He peered down the smoky hallway. No sign of Ivan.

Osborne answered.

"Tell me you've got good news, Flynn."

"I do. The missiles aren't going to be launched today."

"What about the Vice President's daughter?"

"Let's talk later about that—but I think she's still alive."

Flynn ended the call and strained to see through the smoky haze. Still no sign of Ivan.

CHAPTER 64

TODD OSBORNE DIALED HIS PHONE as quickly as his fingers could move. Just under the wire. While the phone rang, he let out a sigh of relief, pleased that Flynn successfully delivered when it mattered most.

"Cuttin' it close, aren't we, Osborne?" Sandford answered.

"Yes, sir. But I've got some good news for you."

"Oh?"

"Yes, I just got a call from our operative and he's disabled the missiles."

"What about my daughter?"

"She's alive, sir."

Sandford paused. "That's really odd because I just got this text with a picture of her lifeless bloody body with a message that says, 'You failed.'"

"That can't be, sir. I just spoke with our operative."

"Well, he's lying to you."

"So you're still going to do what they want you to do?"

"No, I'm not doing what they want me to do—I would've done this any way. It's time that Russia be held accountable for what it's done to me and my family—and the rest of the world."

"Sir, please don't do this. Millions of innocent people are going to die."

"Good-bye, Osborne."

Sandford ended the call. Osborne tossed his phone onto his desk. He needed a miracle.

***

SANDFORD DIALED STRATEGIC COMMAND. He didn't wait for an answer.

"Do it!" Sandford said. "Launch the missiles now!"

Nothing.

"Hello? Are you there? I said, 'Launch the missiles now!'" Sandford demanded again.

Silence.

"Who is this? Stop screwing around and affirm this order!"

"I'm sorry. Who is this?" came the familiar voice on the other end.

"You know good and well who this is—acting President Gerald Sandford. Now do your job!"

The voice on the other end paused again before speaking. "I'm sorry, sir, but I only take my commands from the President of the United States."

"Who do you think you are?"

"This is General Timothy Hill, sir. I'm sure you remember me— I'm the one you recently relieved from duty."

"Then what are you still doing there? Hand the phone to someone who has some real authority!"

"Sir, I'm afraid I am the ultimate authority here since President Briggs reinstated me a few minutes ago. And we aren't starting a war today, per his orders. Is that clear?"

Sandford slammed the phone down and let out an agonizing scream, which quickly turned to sobbing. Through his bleary eyes, he looked at the picture on his other phone—a horrific image of Sydney. He only had himself to blame—and now he'd surely be able to do nothing about it.

For the next several minutes, Sandford stared at the wall, absorbed in an ocean of regret. *How could I have let this happen? How could I have ever given up looking for Sydney? This is all my fault.* He shuddered to think how his misguided actions had nearly led him to start a war.

Two Secret Service agents knocked as they entered the room. They told Sandford he needed to leave and that they were his escort out of the office. He slipped his phone in his pocket and wondered if he could've done anything more—anything to save his daughter.

CHAPTER 65

THE ALARMS WAILED, piercing the smoke and Flynn's ears. Flynn rushed back into the control room to find Sydney lying in the corner. Dashing over to help her, Flynn eased her back to her feet and led her out of the room. If she didn't want to go with him, Flynn couldn't tell. Her compliance shocked him.

On their way toward the exit, Flynn nearly tripped over Buscape, who lay on the floor gasping for air.

He grabbed Flynn's leg.

Flynn stopped.

"This isn't over," he mumbled in a raspy voice. "You'll see. We'll win, eventually."

Flynn paused to pity the man, if only for a moment. The feeling left as quickly as it came, once he remembered the evil this man had propagated.

"It won't be today."

Whooosh!

Suddenly the room was engulfed in more flames. Flynn pulled free from Buscape, leaving him to die. Hoisting Sydney across his shoulder, Flynn hurried down the hallway through a thick blanket of smoke and distanced himself from the inferno as quickly as possible.

They rounded a corner before a large explosion rocked the building again.

After ambling through the building for several minutes, Flynn found the exit he was looking for—a small side exit he remembered being on the building's plans. It appeared to be built for such a time as this, serving as an escape hatch that led them a quarter of a mile away from the building and deeper into the Urals.

Flynn allowed Sydney to go first. Crawling on her hands and knees wasn't easy, given her injury. Every few feet, she winced with pain. Flynn felt sorry for her on one level, for he was the one who inflicted such misery upon her. But on another, no remorse. Sydney made her own decisions, one of which was to align herself with an extremist group of communists bent on causing destruction to the world in an effort to establish communism worldwide. It went against everything Flynn believed, even if a more cooperative humanity seemed like a better world. He just knew such ideals rarely escaped the incubation of the mind's inception. The real world contained vile agents of corruption, distorting good ideas and turning them into the seeds of hatred and violence. True peace would never be obtained through the violent will of a few being imposed on the rest of the world. Yet Sydney once believed this— whether she still did or not made no difference to Flynn. He simply wanted her out of there so she could have a chance to decide for herself.

For fifteen minutes they crawled. Flynn continued behind her, dragging his pack with his foot. They edged their way down the chute until they finally arrived at the doorway to the outside. It too had a keypad, requiring a retinal scan.

Without a word, Sydney put her eye in front of the scanner and waited. The scanner whirred and hummed for a few seconds until finally—*click!* The door lock released and opened slightly into the woods. Sydney crawled out first and stood up before collapsing. Flynn followed, scrambling over to where she had fallen on the forest floor.

Flynn's eyes struggled to see in the cold darkness. He located a small light in his pack to be able to examine Sydney more thoroughly. He then dug out a tightly packed emergency blanket for her. During the day, the blanket's silvery shimmer would reflect light and make them a target. But at night, it was safe. And Flynn knew if they wanted to stay alive, they needed to get out of the Urals as soon as possible.

Noticing a few more spots where Sydney's wound began to ooze, Flynn administered some more pain medicine after re-cleaning the area with an anti-septic wipe. Sydney remained calm and quiet, refusing to say the first word to Flynn. After ten minutes of him fussing over her, Sydney finally uttered something: "Thank you." She then fell back down onto the forest floor in search of some much-needed sleep.

Flynn wanted to call Osborne again, tell him what happened. But it would have to wait until the morning, until he and Sydney were safe, until they both escaped Russia without being detected. He looked around and found a cave nearby where they could seek shelter for the night. They would have to leave early in the morning, as the area would likely be crawling with Russian soldiers looking for the cause of such blasts in the middle of the night.

In the cave, Sydney nestled next to him in an effort to keep warm. She cried quietly, saying nothing. Flynn decided to let it go—let her purge whatever pent up emotions she had built for the past fifteen years.

As he lay down on his back, he heard the distant cry of a wolf. Flynn didn't even jump. If he'd made it through this mission successfully without getting killed, he wasn't going to lose any sleep over wolves.

CHAPTER 66

THREE DAYS LATER, Flynn awoke in his familiar Washington hotel. The Liaison always provided him with superb customer service and a good night's sleep. His stay this time was no different. It was imperative that he received a good night's sleep and why he insisted on the CIA putting him up there. Flynn wanted to look his best when he met President Briggs.

In the downstairs lobby, Osborne waited for him. Flynn chuckled when he thought about how this was as it always was—Osborne sitting around while someone else did real work. But Flynn needed Osborne along with all the intel and gadgets to help him achieve a successful mission. Without the proper equipment and devices, Flynn would have failed. Yet he didn't. And Osborne came off looking like the smartest man in American intelligence.

During the drive to the White House, Flynn stared aimlessly out the window from his backseat position. He noticed the people marching to jobs, some of them undoubtedly spies, agents and operatives. It wasn't easy protecting the world from chaos and mayhem. It took training, skill, and sometimes luck. Flynn considered just how much good fortune he had on his latest mission, concluding it was just as equal to his misfortune. In the end, the balance of the scale didn't matter—only the results did. Millions of people would not die and neither would the President.

***

AWAY FROM THE AUSPICES of the press, President Briggs welcomed Flynn and Osborne into his office for a private meeting. A debt of gratitude this big needed to be paid in person.

"Mr. Flynn, I can't thank you enough for what you did for me and this country," Briggs began. "I know you may have felt like we turned our back on you in the past, but what you just did for the United States—for me—you deserve an apology for how you were treated."

Flynn nodded. "Thank you, Mr. President. I appreciate the sentiment. I've never had anything but pride in my heart for this country. If that wasn't evident before, I think you know that. It was that same pride that made me ashamed when some of our men weren't honoring this great nation the way they needed to."

"I understand," President Briggs responded. "I'm going to have your file expunged and make sure you get the Intelligence Star—and your former boss will be the one to present it to you in a ceremony in front of the entire agency."

Flynn laughed nervously. "I don't think that's necessary, Mr. President. I appreciate the sentiments, but I was just doing what I was asked. I don't really want any attention over all this."

"Very well, then," President Briggs answered. "But there's someone else in this equation who needs to be rewarded—and that's you, Mr. Osborne."

Osborne politely nodded and thanked the President.

Before the meeting concluded, Osborne was informed that he would be given full command of a special black ops unit with unlimited funding, and completely autonomous from the CIA. He would have the authority to investigate and pursue anything he deemed necessary within the country's national security interests. Osborne confessed to Flynn that he hoped for a promotion—but this was far better than anything he could've imagined.

As their time drew to a close, Flynn spoke up.

"Mr. President, there's just one more thing I want to talk to you about," Flynn said.

"Oh, what's that?"

"It's about your Vice President, Gerald Sandford. I've heard rumors that he might be indicted for his actions."

President Briggs nodded, affirming the rumors.

"I'm just going to ask that you don't do that—as a special favor for me."

"And why should I overlook his treasonous acts? For goodness sake, he almost launched another world war while I was incapacitated—and he did it against my wishes."

"I understand how you might feel, Mr. President, but I think you might want to consider just what a difficult situation he was in and how terrorists blackmailed him. I'm not a parent myself, but I can empathize with a parent who was pushed into a corner and felt compelled to do whatever it took to save his or her child. Can't you?"

The President dropped his head and stared at his feet for a few moments before speaking.

"Mr. Flynn, your objection has been noted. I'm not sure how it will play out, but you're a bigger man than I am—a man to whom I owe my life. Thank you for your service."

Flynn and Osborne thanked the President again and exited the room.

On their way out, Flynn filled Osborne in about the CIA's leak—a Mr. Livingston. Osborne promised to look into it and told him not to worry about it any longer.

Then Flynn excused himself. He needed to make a phone call.

"Hello? Is that you, Flynn?" Natalie asked.

"Yes, I made it back alive."

"And you're a national hero—though I doubt anyone will know about it."

"Not unless you tell them."

"Your secret is safe with me."

"And how are you?"

"I'm good—I'm alive. I'm not sure if I'm cut out for this spy life. I think I've had enough excitement for a lifetime."

"Well, I'm just glad everything worked out all right. Now it's time to celebrate."

"Let me guess, Georgia Brown's tonight at eight?"

"Sounds like a plan to me."

Flynn hung up and smiled. At least there was one sane woman in his life.

250 | R.J. PATTERSON

***

FLYNN REMAINED IN WASHINGTON for two more days. He performed a few follow-up interviews for a story his editor Theresa demanded and sought to bring closure to the harrowing turn of events that led him to discover one of the darkest secrets in American history: the group responsible for the assassination of President John F. Kennedy. Yet that story seemed like a simple tale compared to the one he just lived.

Between interviews with officials at the U.S. State Department, Flynn walked by an office with a news program running. On the screen was Gerald Sandford with his wife, sitting next to their daughter, Sydney. The type across the bottom portrayed a far different story than the one he knew to be true: Vice President's Daughter Escapes Russian Terrorists in the Ural mountains.

All three of the Sandfords were crying—an emotion that even affected the interviewer. The staffers gathered near the television also appeared moved by what they saw and heard on the screen.

Flynn shook his head and marched on. It was a happy little ending, but it wasn't the truth—the thing he cared the most about. The Sandfords' version only masked the reality of what happened. Eventually, the truth would come out. But someone else could do it. He had other stories to tend to.

Flynn's phone buzzed with a text message. It read:

Call the office ASAP. Big lead on a story in New Mexico.

Flynn smiled. "It never ends, does it?" he muttered to himself.

ACKNOWLEDGMENTS

NO WRITER CAN EXIST in a vacuum. And this project proved to be one that required the assistance of plenty of people.

For starters, without readers who have found my work—and enjoyed it—I never would have trudged on with the arduous task of writing a novel. Just knowing that you're all out there and enjoying the diversions created by my books inspires me to press on and work diligently to refine my craft.

None of this novel could have been fleshed out the way it was without the guidance of Steven Hamilton, who steered me in the direction of one of the most fascinating characters who emerged from the JFK assassination investigation. His help along with that of fellow archives employees, Amy DeLong and Mary Kay Schmidt, proved invaluable in helping mix fact with fiction.

Pieter VanBennekom provided excellent fodder as someone who actually pursued some of the more mysterious elements of the JFK assassination as a journalist. His stories are deserving of a book.

Jennifer Wolf's editing helped make this a better story. Without her, this novel might be more confusing, not to mention full of female characters wearing horribly matched clothes.

Darrell Chatraw helped craft some of the aviation scenes, lending credence to dogfight descriptions from a veteran of the cockpit.

Though my Russian is all but non-existent, Lesy Chatraw helped me craft some strong phrases throughout the book.

Dan Pitts crafted and conceived the cover, which exceeded any expectations I had in stealing design elements from the original Warren

Report. It's sheer genius.

Bill Cooper continues to produce stellar audio versions of all my books — and have no doubt that this will yield the same high-quality listening enjoyment.

And last, but certainly not least, I must acknowledge my wife and her gracious soul for allowing me to travel across the country and obsess about the JFK assassination for nearly a year as I wrote this book.

ABOUT THE AUTHOR

R.J. PATTERSON is an award-winning writer living in southeastern Idaho. He first began his illustrious writing career as a sports journalist, recording his exploits on the soccer fields in England as a young boy. Then when his father told him that people would pay him to watch sports if he would write about what he saw, he went all in. He landed his first writing job at age 15 as a sports writer for a daily newspaper in Orangeburg, S.C. He later earned a degree in newspaper journalism from the University of Georgia, where he took a job covering high school sports for the award-winning *Athens Banner-Herald* and *Daily News*.

He later became the sports editor of *The Valdosta Daily Times* before working in the magazine world as an editor and freelance journalist. He has won numerous writing awards, including a national award for his investigative reporting on a sordid tale surrounding an NCAA investigation over the University of Georgia football program.

R.J. enjoys the great outdoors of the Northwest while living there with his wife and four children. He still follows sports closely.

He also loves connecting with readers and would love to hear from you. To stay updated about future projects, connect with him over Facebook or on the Internet at www.RJPbooks.com

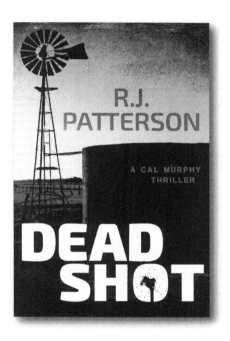

Working as a journalist at a small weekly paper in rural Idaho, Cal Murphy begins losing his big city dreams of writing for a metro paper before his passion is reignited after three high school star athletes are found dead in a 24-hour period.

As he and fellow photographer Kelly Mendoza attempt to make sense of bizarre circumstances that led to the teens' deaths, Cal makes a chilling discovery, uncovering a vast conspiracy that grows darker with every twist and turn.

With a mastermind determined to silence Cal and Kelly for good, the young reporters ultimately must decide if their lives are worth the risk to reveal the truth.

AVAILABLE at Amazon.com